Cascades

General Editor: Geoff Fox

Tough Luck

Tough Luck

Berlie Doherty

CollinsEducational

An imprint of HarperCollins*Publishers*

© Berlie Doherty 1989

ISBN 0 00 330057 9

First published by The Bodley Head Ltd, 1986
Published in *Cascades* in 1989 by Collins Educational
Reprinted 1991, 1996, 1998, 1999 (thrice)
Printed in Hong Kong

For Jane, with thanks

TOUGH LUCK was born out of a writers' residency I had with Hall Cross Comprehensive School in Doncaster in the snowy spring term of 1986. I suggested to one of my groups, 3P, who spent just over an hour a week with me, that I would like to write a book with them, and in a secret ballot more than 50% of them voted for a book about people like themselves. We worked in small groups and chapter by chapter I consulted the whole class for their approval and suggestions. Eight months after leaving them I finished writing it, having spent many weeks in research and rewriting. My first acknowledgements, then, go to 3P and their English teacher for their enthusiastic support and their lively criticisms and ideas:

Jane Allen, Alan Anderson, Donna Bray, Stuart Brown, Ian Cackett, Rehanna Chaudhary, Jonathan Cuell, Tracy Dodds, Caroline Edwards, Rieta Ghosh, Andrew Ho, Helen Jackson, Elliot Jardine, Clare Jones, Nazir Khan, Heidi Marsh, Nigel Marshall, Katharine Meese, Simone Murrin, Veronica Oates, Gavin Parry, Catherine Rhodes, Matthew Rowbotham, Ciara Seth, Martin Smith, Stephen Smith, Jim Sprack, Lydia Turner, Daniel Vernon, Priscilla Yeung.

I would also like to thank Jennifer Barraclough of Yorkshire Arts Association and Phil Jarrett for setting up the residency; and Liz James, Safuran Ara and the Imam of the Doncaster mosque for talking to me about Islam.

The school, staff and pupils in this book are entirely fictitious.

Chapter One

It's late evening in early January, winter-cold. Mightymouth Mulloney, the school caretaker, makes his last rounds of the school before the start of the new term. The corridors are as quiet as ghosts. He glances briefly into the silent rooms to check that chairs and desks are straight, and goes across the yard to the mobiles. The cleaners have left the blackboard as it was at the end of term – *Merry Christmas 3B* chalked across it in bright red, and, hastily sketched in the corner, a green and white bunch of mistletoe and the words *Joe Bead and Miss Peters*, xx. "Daft twits!" He rubs the board clean and stamps the duster down in its pink chalk-cloud. Then he switches off the light, and pauses for a moment, enjoying the strange peacefulness of the room in the moonlight.

"Circus tomorrow!" he says aloud. "Roll up! Bring in the clowns!" He locks the door, pulling his coat collar up against the smack of cold. "And the lion-tamer, heaven help him."

Banks of dense cloud roll across the moon, and a shiver of sleet like tossed gravel grazes his cheeks. He runs the last few yards to his bungalow.

"*Mum!*" shouted Caroline from the top of the stairs. "Where's my blouse?"

"I don't know and I don't care. And I'm not rushing round looking for it now," her mother shouted back. "I've got to get out in fifteen minutes, and so have you. You were told to get your things ready last night."

"I did. I hung it up. Have you pinched it, Tanya? I'll kill you if you have."

Tanya came out of her room. "It's in Mum's room, if you want to know. Waiting to be ironed."

"But I ironed it last night."

"No, you didn't," said Tanya, smug. "That was mine."

"You brat!" shouted Caroline as her sister ran downstairs. "Why didn't you tell me? Brat! *Brat!*"

1

"Caroline, what is up with you?" Her mother came up, sighing. "You're always like this first day back at school."

"But it took me hours to iron that thing, and she didn't even tell me it was hers. She might have told me."

"You might have looked," her mother reminded her gently. "She's at least two sizes smaller than you. Go on, I'll do it for you. You get your music ready."

"Music?"

"It's Tuesday, remember. French horn day."

"That's all I need. I wish I'd chosen flute, Mum. You shouldn't have let me play French horn just because I wanted to when I was ten. I needed proper guidance. Nobody told me what a fag it would be, carting a French horn all over the place. My arms have stretched, look. Will Dad give me a lift?"

"Your dad had to go early because of the weather. Have you seen it outside?"

"Hey, Mum, great, it's snowing!" said Tanya.

"I know. I've put the wellies in the porch."

"I am not wearing wellies!" shouted Caroline. "No way am I wearing wellies at my age. I wouldn't be seen dead in wellies."

"You're in a mood," her mother said. "Anyone would think you were in love, Caroline Shepherd."

"In love!" Caroline caught sight of her own reflection as she went back into her bedroom, and smiled briefly at it. "Just as if!"

Sprat lay in his warm bed trying to put the laser buzz of his alarm clock and the thought of school out of his mind. He lifted up a corner of the curtain and peeped out. It was snowing! He watched the white flakes land on his window and run softly down the pane, leaving watery trails behind them. He breathed on the glass to make them run faster, pressing his finger down to make warm runways for them. He leaned out of bed to switch off the alarm and his quilt slid on to the floor. The house was silent. His dad must be out already. He put on his dressing-gown and went down to the kitchen, shouting good morning to the budgie on the way past the front room. There was a note propped against the kettle. Underneath where he'd written

Dinner Money the night before his dad had written *Have a great day at school. Don't let the dreaded Miss Grace get you down. Did you do that R.E. project? See you about eight. Dad*

Sprat put some bacon in the microwave and took the top and bottom crusts from the new sliced loaf and plastered them with tomato ketchup. Then he slid the oozing bacon between the slices. He danced round the kitchen with it while the kettle boiled, swallowing his sandwich in lumps. Then he ran upstairs again and had a shower, rubbed his hair dry without combing it, and dressed quickly in the clothes that he and his dad had ironed between them the night before. "I bet there's no other school in the world still wearing uniform," he said to the budgie as he came down again. "What d'you think, Squark? Smart, eh?" He made sure his tie was crooked and his collar up a bit, grabbed the loose change that was lying in the ash-tray on the mantel-piece, and ran out. A few minutes later he came back in again, hunted for his school bag, and ran back out into the snow.

Some time later Twagger woke up. He listened to his dad snoring in the next room, then heard him snort himself awake and lumber down the stairs. He slid out of bed and put his socks and trousers on and followed him.

"Get yourself dressed. You look half-starved," his father growled. He poured himself some tea and trudged back up to bed.

"Isn't it time you was back at that school of yours?" he shouted.

"It might be," Twagger muttered.

"Well, get yourself off there, then. I can't be doing with you round the house all day."

"Don't worry. I'm going." Twagger tipped a pile of washing out of the blue launderette bag, found his shirt, and tried to smooth out the creases with his hands. There was a brown iron-shaped mark on the back from when he'd made the mistake of trying to press it a few weeks ago. He put his blazer on over it. The sleeves were even shorter than they had been before Christmas. He put his trainers on and went out without saying

3

goodbye. His dad would be asleep again anyway.

He trudged down the road, hunched against the cold. The old lady in the end terrace tapped on her front window with her walking stick as he went past. He walked on, head down into the swirl of snow, and didn't stop until he could see the school gates. His stomach tightened with cold misery.

"Tomorrow," he told himself. "I'll go tomorrow." He saw Mr Bead, his form teacher, jump off the bus and slither across the road, dodging the traffic. It was gone nine o' clock. Twagger stepped back so he wouldn't be seen, and as soon as the teacher had gone through the gates he crossed over the road and wandered off in the direction of the Frenchgate Centre. At least it would be warm there, and dry. Maybe he'd feel a bit more like going to school later on.

"Oh, come on!" Mr Bead had begged, his frustration mounting as an unhealthy whirring noise grated from his ice-bound car. "I promise to put the anti-freeze in tonight, if you promise to start within the next three tries." The car coughed with January chill, and refused.

Mr Bead slammed the door, and fastened up his overcoat. His bag was heavy – he'd brought far too much work home during the Christmas holidays – and hadn't marked most of it, either. He skidded the half-mile down to the bus-stop. "Good job I didn't say I'd pick Liz up this morning. Good job I decided to set off early to get some work sheets ready." His bus passed him, whooshing sludge into his eyes and hair. "Good job it's my old coat."

He had twenty minutes to wait. By the time he reached school it was nine o'clock. He raced across the road, just catching sight of the thin lad skulking by the gates. Something triggered in his mind, but he didn't have time to let it register. He pounded up the stairs and into the staff-room, flung off his wet coat and draped it over the radiator, knocking someone's steaming glove down the back. He had to dry his hands on his handkerchief.

"Mr Bead!"

He jumped.

4

The practised authority of that voice always made him feel as if he'd just been caught out doing something unspeakable.

"I'd like to talk to you about a boy in your form who made a habit of missing my lessons throughout last term."

"Oh. Twagger."

Miss Grace scooped the bulging teabag out of her cup and put it next to his coat to dry till break.

"Whatever his name is. Michael Sanders. It mustn't happen again, Mr Bead."

"All right, Miss Grace. I'll chase him up again." He watched the grey bobbing bun retreat. Her voice snapped with the rhythm of her shoes. "Indeed, again, Mr Bead. Indeed, again."

In her cold, dark room Mrs Heaton lay and listened to the ticking of her clock. She'd heard children running down the road, shouting with excitement, and she knew that school had started again and that it was snowing. She slid her legs painfully across her bed and felt around with her feet for her slippers. She heaved herself up with her sticks and hobbled out to the kitchen. Snow covered her little garden already.

"Lovely!" she said. "Always lovely, every time."

She put the kettle on and heaved herself back into the room where she lived and slept, and which led out into the street. It took her a long time to get the front door open, as she had to balance her sticks against the walls to get her hands free, and prop herself up with her shoulder. Snow skittered across her face as at last the door swung back.

"Look at that," she said. "Stupid man. Look at that." The milkman had left her bottle on the path instead of on the step. It was impossible for her to reach it without risking the snow. She decided against it, after repeated attempts to lever herself forward and hook it with her stick.

"It'll just have to stay there till Caroline comes, if she comes at all," she said. She closed the door again and swung herself back round into the room.

It was when she passed the window that she saw Twagger, the thin lad from up the street, letting himself out of his front door. "He could get it for me," she thought. She swung her stick up and tapped it on the glass to attract his attention, but he was deep in thought, hunched up and pinched with cold, and he strode past without even looking up. Mrs Heaton sank back on to her chair, frustrated and exhausted with her efforts.

"I'll let you have a cup of tea in a minute," she told herself. "That'll cheer you up, love, milk or no milk."

By mid-day the snow was settled and heavy, the sky was thick and ocean-grey with it. A Boeing lumbered out of the clouds towards Heathrow airport. It approached the runway guided by lights from the ground. Among the passengers was a girl from Pakistan, Nasim. She sat, tight and afraid, while the plane made its bumpy landing, then followed the other passengers out to the airport bus and into the entrance. She was bewildered and tired, and the stinging blizzard frightened her a little. She had heard of snow in England but now that she'd seen it, it was cold, wet stuff that clung to her hair and her eyelashes. She shivered as she waited for her luggage, glad at least of the woollen coat that her mother had bought for her to wear over her shalwar-kameeze. She didn't understand the customs officer who spoke to her. His English was far too fast. She followed the chattering groups again, too scared to look for a trolley for her heavy luggage, confused by the pale and indistinguishable faces of the English travellers, and by the rapid prattle of their voices.

"I must be brave," she thought. "For my mother, I must be brave."

So it was that when at last she came through the barrier into the arrival lounge and saw her brother Majad and her Uncle Assan waiting for her, she let her tears go but she smiled too. Majad, taller than when she had last seen him, a bearded man now, bent down to greet her.

"You will be very happy here, Nasim," he promised her. "I have found a very nice school for you near our home. Hill Bank Comprehensive School."

Hill Bank. Nasim let the name sound in her head. Hill Bank School.

She would not allow herself to think of Pakistan again. She had a new home now.

Chapter Two

Mr Bead pushed his way through the noisy, dawdling groups in the corridor and went across to the mobile. "He's coming!" someone shouted. He grinned to himself.

"Yes, he's coming. Swallow your bubble-gum, everyone. Right. Had a good holiday?"

"Yes, Sir. Did you? Had your hair cut, Sir? It suits you."

"Thank you Donna."

"I had mine permed, and it's all dropped out with the snow. It's a right mess."

Caroline brought him the register. "Did you get anything nice for Christmas, Sir?"

"A new watch," he told her. "Look. It plays a tune too."

"Can't be much good, Sir. You're twenty minutes late already."

He bent down and skimmed through the register. "Everyone here?"

"Yes," they chorused.

He straightened up and counted heads. "One missing," he said.

"Twagger," said Sprat. "What a big surprise."

Mr Bead frowned. "I'm sure I saw him a few minutes ago, by the gates. Where's he got to?"

"Twagging," Sprat told him. "He loves school, Sir."

Mr Bead closed the register. The bell rang for the end of registration and the class started to move out for Art and Metalwork. "Hang on a minute," he said. "I want a word first. Sit down."

He sat on his desk while he waited, watching the blur of snow outside. This time yesterday, he thought, I was still in bed. Caroline looked at Susan. "We're in for it," she said. He always tried to look relaxed when he wanted to have a crack at them. Susan leaned forward and whispered "Have you noticed his shirt's too tight? One of his buttons is going to pop off in a minute!"

"Too much beer!" Caroline laughed.

7

"Caroline!"

"Sorry, Sir."

"Right," said Mr Bead. "You've had a term to get to know each other. You should just about know each other's names by now."

Sprat looked at Martin, who always sat next to him. "Who are you?" he asked.

"I dunno," said Martin.

"O.K." Mr Bead said. "I don't have to tell you that you're a really nice class. The nicest form I've had, in fact...."

"Yes, we will do our Geography homework," Sprat promised. "Can we go now, Sir?"

"Shut up," said Donna. "You can see he's trying to tell us something. Go on, Sir."

"I want you all to make a special effort with Michael Sanders. All right, listen. I know he's difficult. We all know he's difficult. But if you give him a bit of encouragement he'll find it easier to settle down to school again. He's going through a bad time."

"I think his mum's left home, Sir," said Donna.

Sprat flashed her a look of contempt. "Poor little babby," he crooned. "Poor little Mummy's little duckling."

"That's all," Mr Bead sighed. "Scram."

"Any chance of school finishing early?" asked Martin. "Star headlines. Snow Causes Traffic Chaos. Perhaps we should leave now."

"I said scram!"

But by the end of the morning all such thoughts had been abandoned. Someone set up a rumour that the third years were going to make an igloo at dinner-time. Nobody knew who first thought of it. The slow drift of huge flakes gradually grew faster and thicker as the morning wore on. It was difficult to concentrate on lessons with all that going on outside the windows. They watched it settling on their field and for the first time in their lives they weren't praying for the school to close early so they could all go home.

The last lesson of the morning was Maths with Mr Brown, who was also head of third year. He scraped his wellingtons on the step as he came in, and then took them off at the back of the classroom and walked to the front in his socks, leaving a line of sweaty footmarks across the floorboards. Sprat had just stuck his hand through the prised-up window to scoop up a handful of snow to lob at Caroline.

"Shut that window!" Mr Brown snapped at him.

"Sorry, Sir."

Sprat's fingers were trapped. He couldn't release the snow. He drew his hand back in and nursed the little icy lump in his fist till it burned hot and ran melted down his trouser leg.

Caroline hadn't seen Mr Brown come in, and was sitting with her back to the board, talking to Susan and Donna.

"Miss Shepherd, is that the back of your head or have you got hair all over your face?"

He smiled to himself as some of the class tittered and Caroline turned round to face him.

"Ah!" he said. "You *have* got a face."

"That's the back of her head," someone muttered. "She's going bald, like you." It wasn't quite loud enough for Mr Brown to hear.

"Quiet!" He shouted into the muffled giggles. "Get your books out. Let's start as we mean to go on. Blow your noses first. If you haven't got a handkerchief then borrow someone else's. If there's one thing I can't stand about you lot, it's your snotty snouts."

The lesson continued in silence.

When at last the bell went they raced outside, skidding all in a line along the sticky patch by the mobiles. Those who'd brought sandwiches for lunch swallowed them whole, and the others skipped dinner.

The field was full of third years all behaving like little kids, standing with their faces up to the sky and their mouths wide open to drink the flakes; shoving snow down each other's trousers and socks and shirt necks. Twagger had come into school for his dinner. Attracted by the shouting and laughter he wandered into the field and stood watching. A snowball hit him full in the face, and he rubbed it off with the back of his sleeve and stuck his hands deep in his pockets, allowing the snow to settle on his hair and shoulders. Susan, a noisy fair-haired girl, seemed to be in charge of everything. She organised some groups into snow-rolling, and other groups into spreading the rolls of snow out into a circle, and, as more and more third years came to join in, the snow circle grew wider; and little by little, it started to grow in height too.

"Maybe it will keep on and on snowing, and we'll keep on and on building, and our igloo will end up bigger than the mobile!" she told her workers.

This gave Sprat an excuse to stop for a rest. He sat back on the snow wall. "Let's ask Beady if we can have lessons in it."

"I bet even Twagger would want to come to lessons if we had them in here," said Caroline. She looked across at Twagger, bent and scowling, just on the edge of the crowd of third years, not helping, not separate, part of it all and part of nothing.

"Come and give us a hand, Twagger," she shouted to him. He turned away, staring up the field as if he hadn't heard her, his face pinched white with the cold.

"The abominable snowman!" someone giggled.

It was hot work. Soon they were shedding scarves and coats, draping them on the fourth years who were standing round watching, or piling them on bags, or just tossing them out onto the snow. They didn't care. They had a job to do.

"I wonder how often Eskimoes make igloos?" Sprat had found an excuse for another rest. "I mean, do they have one igloo for life or do they have to build a new one every winter? Or do they buy igloos already made?"

"Come on, Sprat. You're just wasting time" Caroline said.
1 "I'm not. I'm thinking. I mean, what do the Eskimo pensioners do? I can't imagine my grandad doing this."

Ian straightened up and took his glasses off to wipe away the steam. "Eskimoes dig the snow out in blocks. There's a lot of it there," he said, and started work again.

"They must be daft, then," said Sprat. "They ought to get someone to invent bricks for them."

Long chains of snow collectors spread out across the field, rolling in to the centre. The workers were spread out along both sides of the igloo, and soon the people working on the outside could no longer see the ones on the inside, only the tips of their fingers as they smoothed down the inner slope. They could see the steam of their breath rising. It was time to shape the roof.

"This is the tricky bit," Ian said. "Take it steady."

There wasn't much talking going on now. They were intent on their work, heaving and rolling, patting and packing, sucking smarting fingers. It seemed as if they'd been doing this for ever, and that there was no other work in life beyond this bending and lifting, bending and lifting.

The fourth years stood in a line, chattering and watching. They didn't join in, didn't even ask to. This was for the third years. Fifth years jeered and sent snowballs skimming and skittering across the field, cheering when they struck their targets. Nobody cared. They were in a frenzy to get it finished before afternoon school; that was all they could think about.

The fifth years cheered again when the bell went. They ran past, kicking out their legs against the igloo walls, sending a volley of snowballs through the little doorway. But the roof was on now. The igloo was made, and stood firm. One by one Mr Bead's class went back in, running backwards so as not to lose sight of it, admiring its smoothness. A handful stayed back just to finish patting down the doorway.

Caroline crawled inside on her hands and knees. It was cool and dark and quiet, like a church.

"See you in the mobile," Sprat called in.

"Let's stay," whispered Susan, crouching in after her.

"Better not," she whispered back. "But we could stay for a bit after school."

"Everyone'll want to then." Susan giggled. "We'd never all fit in. Our breaths would melt it."

"Well, you could stay. It was your idea."

"No, it wasn't," she said. "I just felt like bossing people."

It seemed that after all it was nobody's idea, that the thing had been born from nothing. An hour and a half ago there hadn't been an igloo, and now there was, possessing their field like an alien invasion, and their minds, too. Caroline crawled out after Susan and raced her back to the mobile, and held the quietness of the igloo in her head all afternoon.

There was a row in afternoon registration because Twagger was missing again. "He was out on the field a bit ago, Sir," Donna said. "But he just hasn't come in with us."

"I don't suppose any of you made an effort to talk to him?" Mr Bead said. "It wouldn't have hurt you."

"I did," said Caroline. "He just ignored me." For some reason Mr Bead seemed to be sorry for the lad. None of the other teachers had any time for him. None of the kids did, for that matter.

Caroline caught Susan's eye and sighed. They were sick of being blamed for Twagger's behaviour.

"He just doesn't like us. We can't help it if he doesn't like us."

"And he hates Geography," said Donna. "He won't turn up. I should forget about him, Sir."

Mr Bead sighed. Teachers hate to be beaten. "I'm not starting this lesson without him," he said at last. "Stuart. Go and find him, will you."

"Me, Sir? Do I have to, Sir?"

"Yes, Stuart." Mr Bead sat down and took out his marking. "You have to."

Stuart slouched out of the classroom. Mr Bead carried on with his marking.

"He's going thin on top," Caroline thought, watching him as he bent his head over the books. "I've never noticed that before."

Everyone was whispering and giggling and flicking things at each other and suddenly Susan sent her chair screeching back and ran over to the window. "Look!" she shouted. "I'll kill him!"

She ran out down to the door and Mr Bead snatched at her as she pushed past him. "What d'you think you're doing?" he shouted.

"Let me go, Sir, please!" she shouted back. "It's serious. Someone's kicking our igloo down!"

"Sit down!" said Mr Bead wearily. *"Sit   down!"* as everyone crowded over to the window. "I don't care who's kicking your igloo down. I've got a lesson to get on with so *sit down!*"

"But you said you wouldn't start without Twagger, Sir," said Donna. "And look at him, out there. Look at him!"

"I'll smash his face in!" shouted Sprat. Mr Bead put his hand on his shoulder and held him away at arm's length, Sprat's fists flailing out uselessly.

"Sit down!"

"But Sir, we spent all dinner time making it – we can't just let him kick it in like that."

Mr Bead stood with his back to the door, arms folded. The class shuffled back to their seats in silence, angry at him.

"Hey, guess what!" There was a shout from outside and Mr Bead staggered forward as Stuart pushed open the door. "Some thick'ead's kicking in our igloo!"

His words were drowned out as everyone surged forward, pinning Stuart and Mr Bead against the wall.

"Sit down! Come back!" Mr Bead's voice could just be heard as they raced across the field, driven by anger and excitement and the urge to show him why they all hated Twagger so much.

"Oi," shouted Sprat. The lad booting in the igloo gave a last jeer and drove his foot into the already crumbling pile, and as he slithered away across the snow two more lads leapt out from the back of it and raced after him. Sprat skidded across the field and brought one of them down.

"I don't believe it! They're fifth years!"

Mr Bead teetered over to them in his slippery shoes and held the two fighters apart.

"It's war now," Sprat hissed.

"Ah. Did we break your little wendy-house?" crooned the fifth-year.

"Go!" roared Mr Bead.

"It wasn't a wendy-house. It was a feat of engineering," said Ian. "Bet you lot couldn't do it."

"And now it's ruined," said Susan. "All that work!" She felt like kicking the lad herself.

"We could build it up again after school," Donna said.

Sprat groaned. "Do we have to!"

"We're not leaving it like that. Look at the state of it."

They gazed at the dome of snow with the roof and the sides caving in, and as they watched it it seemed to heave.

"It's moving!" "Someone's in it!"

The snow heaved again, and first a foot, and then a hand, and then a shoulder appeared.

"Mr Bead!" shouted Stuart. "I've found Twagger for you!"

Mr Bead and Stuart heaved Twagger out as if they were hauling a grunting beast out of the river. He shook the snow off himself like a dog, scooping it out of his pockets and his hair and his ears, soaked to the skin. Even Mr Bead laughed. Twagger scowled, then a pleased grin spread across his face. "I forgot my book, Sir," he said.

"Right," said Mr Bead, all his puffed-up anger drained away. "Let's get in, sit you by the radiator and start the lesson, shall we?"

But before the class went in they kicked the igloo down, smashed it in with their feet and their hands, their loud shouts echoing across the field like birds' cries, till there was nothing left of it; nothing for anyone else to take away from them.

Chapter Three

"I want you to write about a nuclear holocaust," said Miss Peters. It was an English lesson late on Thursday afternoon, nearly dark already in a day that had hardly become light. Miss Peters was standing with her back to the class, staring out at the ice-bound field, the death-slide gleaming between the dark buildings, the roofs of distant houses humped under snow-shrouds. She held her arms folded and her shoulders hunched in that tense way she had, as if she was always cold.

"Miss, do we have to? It's too hard," moaned Donna.

"You're old enough to think about these things." Miss Peters didn't turn round. "Thirteen."

"Fourteen."

"Fourteen, then."

"They do the nuclear holocaust in the fifth year," said Stuart. "Our David's doing it. They get films and books and that."

"Could we do a tropical island instead, Miss?" Donna suggested. "I could do that, lying on the sand, sucking a coconut, watching the palm trees waving over my head . . . ."

"You've been told what to write, now get on with it." She turned away from the yellow–grey scene outside. "Get your books out."

"Are you all right, Miss?" asked Susan. "You look sort of spooky."

"Do I?" Miss Peters laughed, and ran her fingers through her hair. "It must be the weather. No more talking now." She went to her desk and took out her books. She just wanted to get on with marking the fifth-year assignments in peace. She had a meeting to go to at seven, and she'd not slept the night before. If she didn't get them marked today they'd drag over the weekend, and start a pile-up into next week.

"Miss?"

"Yes, Ian?"

"When they write about these things, they always happen in the north of England, have you noticed? Aren't they going to get hit in the south?"

Donna put her pen down. "I feel right depressed now. I'm not doing it."

Miss Peters relented. "All right. I'll change the title to give you more scope. "The Worst Thing That Could Happen to Me." What's the worst thing that could happen to you?"

"Going deaf," said Martin.

"Pardon?" said Sprat.

"You've got thirty minutes left."

At last the class settled down into silence. Miss Peters leaned back, feeling round for the polo mints in her jacket pocket. She could hear the soft swirl of wind outside, and the rapid scrabbling of the children's pens. Someone in the main building was playing a flute, like rippling, cold birdsong. She slid the polo mint in her mouth and caught Twagger's eye. She smiled at him and he stared back, unblinking. "He's like a turnip," she thought. "I bet if I cut him open he'd be the same all the way through."

Sprat spread out his long legs into the aisle, kicking over someone's sports bag. "And he's like a runner bean. The tough and stringy sort. What's Donna?" She started sketching them down the side of her marks book. "A nice bubbly cauliflower. Caroline ought to be a carrot with that hair, but she's too thoughtful and interesting for a carrot. Red cabbage."

"How d'you spell psychopath, Miss?" asked Martin.

"You're a tomato," she thought, surprised.

"T.W.A.G. . . ." whispered Sprat.

"It starts with p s y. Look it up." She saw herself as she'd been after Joe Bead had left her last night, when he'd told her that he was thinking of moving away.

"I'm an onion," she said out loud.

"What did you write about?"

Sprat was waiting at the school gates for Caroline, as usual. He always waited till the other lads had gone before he caught up with her, and she used to hang round the cloakrooms to give him time, though they never arranged to meet.

"Oh, hi, Sprat. I wrote about old Mrs Heaton. I think it must be terrible for her, being all crippled like that. I hope it never happens to me."

"Who's Mrs Heaton?"

"You know," said Caroline. "She's my Saturday job."

"Oh, aye. Your good deed."

"She's not a good deed. She's a friend. She lives near my grandma's and she asked her if Helen and I could push her down to the Frenchgate on a Saturday. I really like her."

"Does she pay you?"

"Course she does. It's a job, like babysitting. But I sometimes go when it's not my job. I told Mum I'd call in there tonight to see if she wants any bread. We couldn't take her last Saturday because of the snow. Come with me if you like."

"D'you think I've gone soft or something? I can't be bothered with old people. They talk too much."

"Just you wait till you're an old man. You'll be glad of someone to help you out then."

"I'll do it myself first," Sprat said. "I don't want anyone running round after me."

Caroline stopped and looked up at him. "You're a big poser, d'you know that? A big spidery poser."

He laughed, his voice breaking through several octaves on its way out.

"*And* you sound like a donkey. What did you write about, anyway?"

Sprat shrugged. His feet teetered out to the sides as they stepped onto a slippery part of the gutter. "Something that's already happened."

"What?"

"Someone having a baby."

"What?"

"You know. My so-called mum."

Sprat's mother had left home during the summer, and Sprat hadn't seen her since. He and his dad had heard at Christmas that she'd had a baby, and they'd never even seen it. He still found it hard to talk about her. He hated her, or so he said.

"I'm sorry. I forgot."

He shrugged again. He had a photograph of his mother behind his gold-fish bowl in his bedroom. It distorted her face;

17

he could see it now, in his mind.

"You go in and see your old lady," he said. "I'll wait for you."

"She'll expect me to have a cup of tea with her," said Caroline. "She always does. I might be ages."

"Don't worry. I'll wait." He couldn't explain even to himself why he wouldn't go in with Caroline. He was embarrassed at the thought of talking to someone in a wheelchair. He couldn't imagine himself sitting in front of the fire drinking tea and chatting. They never did that at his house now. And he didn't want any old lady thinking that he was Caroline's boyfriend.

"All right. I'll see you."

Caroline was disappointed. He couldn't help that. Sprat wandered round the back of Mrs Heaton's house and along the entry. He was so tall that he could see over the top of the walls, right into people's kitchens. He saw Caroline filling a kettle at Mrs Heaton's sink, and pulled a face at her. Then he heard a commotion in one of the other yards; two people yelling at each other, and a bin or something being kicked round; someone howling as if they'd been hurt. He raced along the backs, jumping up so he could see into people's yards as he ran, and he was just in time to see a big man in a grubby vest and with his trouser braces hanging down, slamming his kitchen door. A lad was on his knees, clutching his stomach, moaning to himself. He pulled himself up painfully and stumbled back into the house, and the shouting started again, the man's voice raised in a brutal sort of anger, and the boy's voice half-sobbing. Sprat ran back up the entry and banged on the door of Mrs Heaton's house. Caroline was really pleased to see him.

"Sprat's come!" she called to the old lady. "I knew he wanted to come in, really."

Sprat pushed past her into the room where the old lady was drinking tea by the fire.

"Oh, I've heard a lot about you, Sprat," she said. "And do you know, you're even better looking than Caroline said you are. Quite dishy! Look at that lovely thick hair."

Caroline went quickly out of the room. Sprat could hear her swilling her face with cold water in the kitchen.

"Mrs Heaton," he said. "I've come to ask you about the lad who lives two doors up. Do you know him? His name's Twagger."

"Twagger?" Mrs Heaton repeated. "That's an unusual name."

"Michael Sanders," shouted Caroline from the kitchen. She came back in, her hair damp and stringy. "We call him Twagger because he's always missing school. I didn't know he lives round here, Sprat."

"I'm sure it was him," said Sprat. "And if it was, he was being beaten up by his dad."

Mrs Heaton nodded. "I know the ones you mean. I don't know them, of course. I know of them. I've heard them. That man used to knock his wife about till she ran off, God knows where. And now he takes it out on the lad." She sipped her tea noisily and handed her empty cup to Sprat. "To tell you the truth, I feel sorry for all of them. There's a lot of misery going on in that house, if you ask me."

Next morning Twagger was very late coming in to class. It was Maths. He stood outside the door of the mobile, knowing that he'd been seen coming across the field, and knowing the kind of taunting he would get when he went in. He was cold and tired; the bitter wind cut through his thin trousers. He could hear Mr Brown's voice, grinding on with acid insistence: "Wipe your snout, Metcalfe. I've seen pigs with cleaner habits than you...."

Twagger kicked the snow off his trainers and pushed open the door. "Ah," smiled Mr Brown. "Don't look now, but Einstein's just walked in. What an honour. Do sit down." The class laughed. Twagger pushed his hands deep into his pockets and walked to his seat, head down, as if he felt that if he couldn't see anyone no-one would see him.

"You're early, Twagger. It's only half-past nine," said Jonathan.

"Leave him alone," said Caroline.

Twagger sat, rigid, in his chair, not looking at anyone. Some people turned round to laugh at Caroline.

19

"The little lady has a soft heart," said Mr Brown. "But then, that's what little ladies are for, isn't it, Miss Shepherd. Fear not, Sanders. The gorgeous Miss Shepherd is going to fight your battles for you. I bet she's got big biceps too. Show us your biceps, Miss Shepherd."

Mr Brown was in good form, and he was enjoying himself. The class laughed with him as Caroline, scarlet now, bent over her book and pretended to work.

"Done your homework, Sanders?" Mr Brown's voice was casual. Twagger ignored him, humiliated.

"Well?"

Still Twagger ignored him.

"Why, Sanders? Why not? What's so special about you that makes you think you can come and go as you please and do your homework when you feel like it? Stand up!"

Twagger scraped his chair back and stood up, his fingers levering up the edge of his table as if any minute he would tip it up and let it thud to the floor. He'd done that before now.

"Well? What's your excuse this time?"

"An igloo fell on his head sir," said Stuart. The class giggles eased the tension in the room.

Mr Brown smiled again. "You've got snow on the brain then, is that it? Answer me, lout! Or has the snow frozen up your tonsils as well?"

"Leave him, Sir!" Caroline burst out. "It's not fair."

At last Mr Brown established order and the class settled down to work. Twagger didn't sit down again, and Mr Brown didn't ask him to.

They ignored each other. Susan slid Caroline's exercise book towards her and scribbled "Caz loves Twagger" on the back. Caroline smiled and pulled a face at her.

At the end of the lesson Mr Brown told Twagger to follow him to his office. Twagger pushed his way after him down the class and then went across to Caroline's desk. He stood looking down at her till Susan nudged her, laughing, and she glanced up. She flushed. His pale, cold eyes made her feel uncomfortable.

"I didn't ask for your help," Twagger said. "And I can do without it."

"Sorry," Caroline said quickly. "Don't bother to thank me, then."

"I wasn't going to."

"Oi," shouted Sprat. "I'll get you for that, Twagger." His mates roared.

"I feel sorry for you, Twagger," said Stuart. "You're dead meat tonight."

Twagger pushed his way round the chairs till he was standing in front of Sprat's desk. "Go on then," he said. "Hit me. You might as well get on with it."

Sprat shoved his chair back, his temper up. He caught Caroline's eye. "Poser!" she mouthed at him.

"Not here," he said. "Make a mess of the floor."

"Where, then?"

"Forget it. I don't scrap little kids."

"Softy...." breathed Martin.

"If anyone scraps him, it should be Caroline," said Susan. "She doesn't need lads sticking up for her."

"All right," Twagger swung round to face her. "Go on then."

"Don't be daft," said Caroline.

"Go on. Hit me."

The class stood in a ring round Twagger and Caroline and Sprat, and they stared at each other like cats in an alley-way, hating each other.

"Come on," taunted Twagger. "Show us your biceps."

"Go on, Caroline, scrap him," said Susan. "He's asking for it."

"He's used to it," said Sprat slowly. "Aren't you, Twagger?"

Twagger pushed himself suddenly out of the ring, his face twisted up with misery. "Bastard!" he shouted. "Leave me alone! Leave me alone, the lot of you!"

Chapter Four

Mr Bead had just come in. He jerked his head to the door. "Mr Brown's waiting for you, Michael," he said quietly to Twagger. Then he sat down on his desk with his arms folded. One by one everyone went back to their seats. Still he said nothing. Everyone sat in uncomfortable silence, shuffling their feet, and some of the girls giggling a bit out of nervousness, and still Mr Bead said nothing.

It was Jonathan who broke the spell of guilt at last. "Sir," he blurted out. "Don't blame us. It was his fault. He was asking for it."

"He always does, Sir," said Donna.

"I see," said Mr Bead, obviously not seeing at all.

Caroline put her hand up. "Please sir, Sprat and I have got something to tell you. In private, Sir."

Sprat blushed and glared across at her. "Have we?" She glared back at him.

"Right," said Mr Bead. "Let's talk."

He gave the class some work to do then he and Caroline went outside into the yard. Sprat grinned at his mates to hide his embarrassment and followed them.

"Well?" said Mr Bead.

Caroline looked at Sprat. "Go on. Tell him."

"Tell him what?"

"Tell him what you saw last night."

"I didn't have the telly on," said Sprat. "I was playing darts with my dad."

"Tell him!"

"It's cold out here," said Mr Bead. "Is this going to be worth listening to or not?"

"It is important," Caroline told him. "Sprat saw something that you ought to know about."

"I'm not telling him that. I'm not even sure it was Twagger."

"What was Twagger doing?" asked Mr Bead. "Come on, you two. I can't stand the suspense."

"He wasn't doing anything," said Caroline at last. "Sprat

22

saw him being hit by his dad."

"I can't be sure it was him," Sprat insisted. "It was nearly dark."

"And if it was him...." Mr Bead prompted.

"I saw this lad being walloped, Sir," said Sprat. "His dad or whoever it was really laid into him. And Twagger, if it was Twagger...."

"It was," Caroline insisted. "Mrs Heaton said it was."

"Go on."

"Twagger was ... well ... kind of crying." Sprat half grinned at Mr Bead, embarrassed again, and then looked down quickly. "It was bad."

"And yet you still wanted to threaten him this morning," said Mr Bead. "You're nothing but a big lout sometimes, Dowd."

Sprat hung his head. "Sorry, Sir. I wouldn't have touched him, Sir. I feel sorry for him, now, but I still don't like him. I can't help that, Sir."

"I don't like you much, sometimes," said Mr Bead. "But I don't go round threatening you, do I?"

Sprat stuck his hands in his pockets and turned his face away. Mr Bead was his favourite teacher.

"What is it you don't like about Michael Sanders, anyway?"

Sprat shook his head. "Dunno, Sir. None of the kids like him. He won't join in or anything. He just hangs about watching us. He's not like the rest of us."

"He's right sullen," Caroline added. "Moody."

"Did any of you know him from his last school?"

"Don't think so."

"What will you do about him, Sir?" asked Caroline. "Will you report his dad to the police?"

Mr Bead shook his head. "I'm not sure, Caroline. I'll do something, I promise. And meanwhile, I want you two to promise not to say a word about this to anyone else in the class. And to leave Twagger, as you call him, in peace."

"I don't think he'll be back today, Sir," said Caroline.

"No, Caroline. Neither do I." Mr Bead gestured to them

both to go back in with him to the class; and though everyone looked up from their work in hushed expectation, Sprat and Caroline sat down at their desks in silence, solemn with the promise that they'd made to Mr Bead and with the seriousness of the situation.

"Liz," Joe Bead sat next to Liz Peters in the staff room. She made room for him and gave him three segments of her tangerine. "What do you know about Twagger?"

"Michael?" she frowned. "Not much, except I thought he was a turnip and now I think I'm wrong."

Joe laughed. "What happened to change your mind?"

"He's still a turnip, but he's got maggots in. I gave them a piece of writing to do last Thursday, last time he showed up at an English lesson, and he wrote me a really nasty piece. A video nasty, nearly. All about people beating each other up and getting their revenge – all blood and bones all over the place. He's got a good imagination, I'll say that for him."

"Can I see it?"

"I chucked it away, Joe. I won't mark pieces like that. I know they read horror stories, some of them, but I won't let them get away with writing them. Not for me. I'm not interested in that sort of writing."

"He might be trying to tell you something."

"He might be trying to tell me that he's sick."

"No. Unhappy."

Liz rolled up the tangerine peel and aimed it at the wastepaper basket. "Never was good at netball," she laughed, as it hit Mr Brown and he looked up, surprised.

"I'd love to get to know that kid," Joe said.

Mr Brown sat down next to them, and Liz turned away slightly from his rank tobacco smell. She bent down to pick up her drink.

"Is that my cup you're using?" Miss Grace demanded.

A gale of laughter from the modern languages department's bridge clique drowned out Liz's reply.

"Which little monster are we talking about now?" Mr Brown asked. He balanced his coffee cup on his knee while he felt for his cigarettes. "Coffin nail?" he offered the packet to Joe.

"More sense," Joe smiled, shaking his head. "We were talking about Michael Sanders."

"Sweet child," said Mr Brown. He sucked on the cigarette end and drew his lips back over his yellow teeth, inhaling sharply. "Diligent, obliging, a pleasure to teach, and shows some ability."

"That's what I think," laughed Liz Peters. "A real smashing kid."

"I'm serious," Mr Brown told her. "That's the report that came with him from his last school. When did they write that? Last July at the latest."

"So what happened to him?"

Mr Brown shrugged. He drained back his coffee and tapped his ash into the cup. "Usual story. Home life stinks. School stinks. We stink. He stinks. Take your pick. A menu of miseries, Mr Bead. I've heard it all before." The bell shrieked, and he ground the last of his cigarette into his cup. "Bloody bell!" he said, ambling out.

"*He* stinks," Liz said. "What's he doing in this job anyway? He doesn't even like kids."

"It's all show," Joe assured her, winking at Miss Grace, who was improving her face. "Deep down he's passionately fond of children, and much too shy to say so."

"Aren't we all!" agreed Miss Grace. She dabbed a blob of lipstick onto her cold-score scab and smiled lopsided at Joe. "Aren't we all!"

Joe Bead set off for Twagger's house that night after school.

Caroline and Sprat followed him and slipped into Mrs Heaton's house when they reached Twagger's road. Mrs Heaton was surprised to see them two days on the run.

"I see more of you than I do of my own grandchildren," she told Caroline. "And isn't it lovely of you to bring your boyfriend with you! There aren't many lads these days who'd spare the time to have a cup of tea with an old duck like me!"

Sprat groaned and went to put the kettle on. He went out into the yard and strained his ears to listen to what was going on up the backs. He was dying to know what was happening in Twagger's house.

Joe had to knock on the door several times before it was opened. The smell of tobacco smoke and beer rushed out to meet him. Mr Sanders, unshaven and still in his vest and braces, peered out at him.

"Thought you was the telly-man, way you was knocking," he said. "What d'you want?"

"I'm Mr Bead, from Hill Bank School. I'm Michael's form teacher. Can I come in, Mr Sanders?"

"What's he got up to now?" grinned Mr Sanders. "Been knocking teachers about?"

"Can I come in, Mr Sanders?" Mr Bead repeated. He didn't feel much like going in to the stench of that house, but he didn't want to carry on this conversation out in the street either, with a circle of toddlers round his knees.

Mr Sanders went back into the house, and Mr Bead followed him. There was no sign of Twagger. The living room carpet was stained with swirls of alcohol and cigarette burns. In the centre of the room was a wooden coffee-table with two opened beer cans, and a litter of magazines from the job centre. Mr Sanders settled himself on the brown settee, picked up one of the cans, and stretched his feet across the table. In the corner of the room an American film blared on the television. Cars chased each other, screeching, across the screen.

"Mr Sanders," said Mr Bead at last. "I'm very concerned about your son."

"Oh, aye?" The man's eyes flicked across to him then back to the screen. He sucked at the beer can.

"He's not been coming to school, for one thing." Mr Bead had to shout above the loud film track.

"Doesn't like it, probably."

"I'm afraid that doesn't give him the right to miss school," Mr Bead said. He tried to smile. "Don't like it myself, some of the time."

Twagger's dad snorted scornfully. "I'm sorry for you. Don't know you're born, you lot."

"Michael doesn't seem to be very happy at the moment,"

26

Mr Bead tried again. "I was wondering if we could talk about that."

Mr Sanders drained his can noisily. "How d'you mean, talk about it? Talk about what?"

"About Michael, basically. What can you tell me about him that might explain his behaviour at the moment?"

There was a long pause. The front door opened and closed again. Light steps ran up the stairs. "Is that him now?" asked Mr Bead.

"What's he been telling you?" shouted Mr Sanders. "What you come sneaking and prowling round here for anyway? I'm not choosing to tell you anything about my son, because he *is* my son, and because he's no concern of yours."

"Well, he is my concern." Mr Bead was alarmed at the aggression in the other man's voice. "While he's at school and in my form he is my concern."

"And while he's not at school he's mine, and as you've just been telling me that he never comes to school anyway I suggest you get out of here. Now."

He stood up, and Mr Bead jumped out of his chair.

"I'd like to see Michael before I go," he said.

"And I'd like you to shove off now, because you're getting up my nose. Clear off, will you?"

"I'd like your assurance that Michael will be coming to school in future, Mr Sanders." Mr Bead backed down the hall, glancing anxiously up the stairs.

"Don't you worry, he'll be coming to school, if I have to get out of bed in the morning and take him there myself. Now clear off."

He opened the door and Mr Bead plunged out into the wonderful sleety air of the street.

It was nearly dark, but Sprat, sitting in the firelight of Mrs Heaton's front room, saw him hurry past.

"I've got to go now," he said. "Cheerio, Mrs Heaton. Thanks for the char."

"That's what the Chinese call it," said Mrs Heaton. "Char. It's a Chinese word. Great tea-drinkers, the Chinese. Like me!" she giggled into her third cup.

"Come on, Caroline," Sprat mouthed at her. "Beady-Eyes has gone."

Caroline jumped up. "I'll wash the things. I won't be a sec."

Sprat raced up the back entry to Twagger's house. He heard his father shouting, and then he saw a light flick on in an upstairs room. The shouting increased, there was the sound of furniture being knocked about, and Twagger's voice raised too. Then the father's voice was raised in a real fury, and then everything went quiet. The light was switched off, and Sprat ducked as he saw a figure approach the window and pull back the curtains.

Caroline ran up the entry to him. "What's happened?"

"We should never have told Beady, that's what. We haven't made things better for Twagger. We've made them worse."

Chapter Five

It wasn't until half-way through the second week that the new girl arrived. Mr Brown brought her in while Mr Bead was taking form period with the class. They were in the middle of a rowdy discussion on smoking; Mr Bead was doing an imitation of someone with a terrible smoker's cough and he was leaning over the waste paper basket hacking and gasping as if he was trying to cough his toenails up. Mr Brown came in without anybody seeing him.

"Vomiting, Mr Bead?" he bellowed.

The laughter and shouting ended abruptly. Everyone stood up in silence. Tracy hid the waste paper basket under her desk.

"Demonstrating the evils of smoking," Mr Bead said lamely.

Mr Brown strode up to the front of the class. The familiar acrid tobacco smell of his clothes and breath passed with him. Everyone knew his smell. They all hated him to hang over their desks when they were writing. Simone coughed loudly as he passed her.

"Come along, dear. They're not animals, even if they behave like them," Mr Brown said to the door at the back of the class.

Everyone turned round and saw the girl who had followed him in and who now stood behind the class, her eyes cast down. She was clutching a Marks and Spencer's carrier bag with school books in. Her hair was in long black plaits tied with blue ribbons; she wore a brand-new school uniform that was too big for her, with baggy blue trousers underneath her school skirt, and she was dark brown.

"Come here, child," said Mr Brown. She stayed where she was, fumbling and fumbling at the handles of her carrier bag.

"Come along now," Mr Brown said again. Her eyes flicked up to him, terrified, and down again.

Mr Brown raised his eyebrows at Mr Bead. "You've frightened the life out of the girl with all that noise you were making," he said. He lowered his voice slightly. "Never let your class get out of hand, Mr Bead. They don't respect you for it." Mr Bead coughed discreetly behind his hand.

"Right, Three Bead, this is your new classmate. As you can see, she's a foreigner. She's new to England so she doesn't know how you behave. Haven't given her a very good impression, have you?"

"I'm sure she'll get used to us, Mr Brown."

"She'll have to, Mr Bead. Now, as you can see, she's very shy. She understands English, but she doesn't speak it very well yet, do you?" He said this bit slowly, and with his voice raised, as if she was deaf or stupid. The top of her head moved slightly to show that she understood him.

"Right. Well. I'll leave her to you." He strode out, pointing at bits of paper on the floor as he went

Mr Bead went down to her and put a hand on her shoulder. "Come on and meet the class," he said gently. She walked meekly in front of him, head bowed, and stood facing the class.

"Would you like to tell me your full name?" he asked her. The top of her head moved slightly again.

"Baggy Pants!" Susan whispered. The girls on the back row collapsed into helpless giggles.

Mr Bead glanced up from his register and frowned at them. Grins of delight were lighting up the faces of the other girls.

"Tell me your Christian name."

"I not Christian, Sir. Muslim." She whispered. "Sorry."

Even Mr Bead smiled this time. "What are you called?"

"Nasim, Sir."

"Would you like to choose somewhere to sit, Nasim?" he asked.

She flicked her eyes up again, darting anxious glances like a small brown bird round the strange faces, and slumped down next to the only person who wasn't looking at her; Twagger.

"I see," said Mr Bead, pleased. "Perhaps you could look after Nasim, Michael. Show her round the school."

There were hoots of laughter as Twagger pushed back his chair and Nasim jumped up again and ran to the front, clutching her carrier bag to her. "My brother say me I not sit by boy, Sir," she said. "Sorry."

"My brother say me I not sit by Pakki, Sir. Sorry." Twagger mimicked her low bubbling accent.

"Get out!" Mr Bead told him. "And don't come back till you've worked out why that's a very offensive remark."

"But *he's* offended," Donna said. "Fancy her not wanting to sit by a lovely boy like him!"

Twagger pushed back his chair again and walked out through the jeers.

"He wasn't thinking of staying, anyway," said Martin. "He only comes in to get his socks dry."

"Pack it in," Sprat muttered.

Mr Bead asked Nasim to sit at the desk in front of the teacher's table. "No one ever sits there," he told her. "I can't think why."

"She'll get wet there," Susan said. "Mrs Quin sprays everyone when she's doing dictation."

"Talk quietly till the bell goes. I'll have a chat with Nasim."

Mr Bead sat down in the chair next to Nasim. She shrank away from him a little. The shouted remarks of the class alarmed her. Her brown fingers fidgeted nervously on the desk top, reminding Mr Bead of dusty sparrows. She had a faint spicey smell about her. "I'm Mr Bead," he said to her quietly. "I'm the form teacher, and I take you all for Geography as well. I don't teach you today."

"No, Mr Bead."

"Where did you learn English, Nasim?"

"In a place near Mirpur."

"Is that in Pakistan or India?"

"Pakistan, Mr Bead."

"And how long have you been in England?"

"One week."

"It's very cold here."

"Yes. Very cold."

"What is the weather like in Pakistan now?"

"Not so cold." If she closed her eyes she could see grey rain swilling across the fields where the old women shouted to their sheep to drive them down; she could see slack-necked oxen hauling carts through the muddy tracks, and the boys running behind to push the slipping wheels.

"Are all your family here, Nasim?"

"No, Mr Bead."

31

"Who are you living with?"

"My Uncle Assan and my aunt. She is calling Zarniga. And my brother is here and my ... my her children. My uncle children."

"Nieces and nephews."

"Yes. Nees and neff."

"I hope you will be very happy with us, Nasim."

She nodded. The dusty sparrows trembled apart and together again. The sudden blurt of the bell startled her, and she reached down for her bag.

"No, you stay here," he told her. "I have to go and teach another class. What's first lesson, Martin?"

"English, Sir."

"Good." Mr Bead touched Nasim's shoulder as he stood up, and she tensed away from him. "Miss Peters will be in soon, Nasim. She's very nice."

"Yes, Mr Bead."

Mr Bead wasn't surprised to find that Twagger had gone when he left the mobile. He decided to wait in the corridor for Liz Peters to come out of fourth year assembly so he could tell her about Nasim. Sprat skidded up to him just as he reached the main building. "Sir. Can I have a word with you about Twagger?"

"Go on then."

"His dad was having a go at him again after you left the other night."

"How do you know I went there?"

"I've got a friend in his road. I saw you going past."

"O.K. Thanks for telling me." He'd seen Liz Peters coming. She smiled at him through the bobbing heads coming out of the hall.

"What did his dad say?"

"Never mind about that. The best thing you can do is to stick up for him the way you did this morning. Thanks for that."

Sprat nodded and side-slid back across the yard. A clump of ice landed just in front of his feet on the death-slide and sent him staggering forward onto his knees, grazing his palms sharply as he flung his hands out to save himself. He swung himself up in time to see Twagger dodging back behind the building. In a fury he slithered after the lad, caught him up, and pinned him against the wall. Twagger tried to squirm away from him while he jammed ice-lumps down inside his collar.

"That'll do your bruises good!" Sprat called after him as Twagger at last broke away and scuttled across the field, bent and howling like a thin dark dog as he tried to shake the pebbles of ice out of his shirt.

"Are you coming in or not?" Miss Peters called to him from the doorway, and, suddenly ashamed, Sprat followed her into class.

At lunchtime Nasim found herself alone in the classroom. She had no idea what she was supposed to do. She had watched the other children leaving the room in their groups, and had half-stood up to follow them. She sat down again, bewildered, as the last one ran across to the main building without so much as a backward glance at her. At least it was quiet in the room now. She put her carrier bag on her desk and took out her books. She opened her English exercise books and stroked the smooth pages with the back of her hand. Then she began to write down all the new words she had learnt. NEES. NEFF. MISS PETERS. MATHS. When Mr Bead came in just before the afternoon bell to do some marking she was still there. She looked up, pleased to see him.

"Hello, Nassam," he said. He couldn't quite remember her name. "Did you have a good lunch?"

She smiled at him.

"Good girl," he said, and settled down to his work.

Nasim was hungry and tired and her brain was spinning with new words. She had understood little of the day's teaching, and by the middle of the afternoon her head was throbbing and her throat was aching. When the bell went for the end of school the classroom emptied as rapidly as it had done at dinner-time, and once again she was left on her own. She followed the others out into the dull afternoon light and made her way to the front gates of the school, where her brother and uncle were anxiously waiting for her.

"Have you been a good girl?" her uncle asked her, teasing, and she laughed up at him. The two men talked together in Punjabi as they went down the school drive, and Nasim was conscious of the curious glances the children gave them.

When she got home she washed her face and her hands and her feet, glad of the comfort of the warm water, and changed out of her uniform into her favourite citrous yellow shalwar-kameeze with its long dupatta scarf. Her aunt boiled tea, sugar and milk in a pot for her and brought it up to her room.

"Have you had a good day, Sheema?" she asked, using her pet name for her. Nasim nodded. She nursed the warm cup in her hands. "I have homework to do," she said proudly. Her aunt laughed. "I suppose you want me to do all the cooking tonight, then?"

"No, I'll come down and crush the spices for you soon," Nasim promised. "I did some of my work in the middle of the day."

"And you have to take Yasmine for her Qur'an lessons at the mosque," her aunt reminded her. "You look so tired, little Sheema."

"It'll be better soon," Nasim told her. "I'll be very brave and talk to some girls tomorrow."

Her aunt laughed at the thought that lively, talkative Nasim needed to wait a day to talk to someone. "They'll have problems trying to keep you quiet, once you start!"

Nasim didn't talk to any of the girls that week. The teachers were all kind to her and some of them remembered to speak slowly when they were talking to her, though some, like Mr Brown, shouted. Miss Peters always smiled at her and repeated things for her, but Mr Bead was the only one who ever sat down by her when he had set work for the others, and she always shrank away from him. Occasionally someone shouted out a remark to her which she didn't understand but which made everyone else laugh; she burned inside with humiliation, knowing that they must be laughing at her, though she didn't understand why. Most people ignored her, even when she smiled at them, and this was even harder for her to understand.

She spent break and lunchtime in the classroom; if she went outside she stood alone, and she found it difficult to recognise even the children from her own class.

She didn't say anything about all this at home. Her aunt had never been to an English school, neither had Majad or Uncle Assan. How could they imagine what it was like for her? And as for little Yasmine, she had always lived here. She chattered away in English with a broad local accent, and had made dozens of friends at her little local school. Nasim kept her puzzlement and her disappointment to herself, and late at night when the house was quiet and Yasmine asleep beside her she struggled to keep the thoughts of home out of her mind.

"I wish I hadn't come here," she whispered into the silence. "I don't belong."

"How's Nasim getting on?" Miss Peters asked Caroline at the end of the week. Caroline had come across to the stock cupboard with her to help her carry a new set of English books.

"All right," said Caroline. "I think."

"You're all looking after her, then?"

"She ... she likes to be on her own."

"Caroline, you have talked to her, haven't you?"

Caroline shifted her load of books. "I think so."

"You think so!" said Miss Peters. "What on earth's that supposed to mean?"

"I don't know what to say to her, though."

Miss Peters didn't speak to her again till they'd reached the mobile. "I thought I could have relied on you, of all people."

At break Caroline called Susan back. "We've got to talk to her," she said, nodding to Nasim's head, bent over her books.

"Talk to her? What about?"

"You know. Make friends."

Susan giggled and followed her to the front of the room.

"Hello, Nasim," said Caroline.

Nasim looked up, startled, from her writing.

"D'you want to come round the yard with us?"

Caroline rushed it out so fast that Nasim had no idea what

35

she'd said. She shook her head slowly to show she hadn't understood.

"Sorry?"

"It's probably too cold for her outside," said Susan. "Cold?" she said loudly.

"Oh, yes, very very cold." Nasim laughed.

"Come on then," Susan said to Caroline. "We'll go out."

As soon as they were outside they both started laughing, more out of relief and embarrassment than anything else. "She's nice though, isn't she?" giggled Caroline.

"Oh yes, very very," laughed Susan, hardening her r's and smiling widely as Nasim had done. "Very, very nice."

Nasim sat still in her chair and listened to their laughter, and her shame crept through her blood like a small fire.

When lunchtime came Susan pushed Caroline out of the classroom first. "Come on, quick. We don't want her hanging round with us all lunchtime."

"She never has lunch anyway," said Caroline. "I've never seen her in the cafeteria. It must be Ramadan or something."

"What?" Susan laughed. "Ramawhat?"

"You know. We've done it in R.E. When they don't eat or drink anything for a whole month."

"Don't be daft," said Susan. "They'd die."

"Something like that, anyway," Caroline shrugged. "Come on, let's run or we'll never get in the queue."

Twagger was back in school that day, and was the last to leave the mobile. He looked over Nasim's shoulder to see what she was writing.

"What you doing that for?" he asked.

She put her pen down and stared at her paper.

"Can't Pakki's talk to boys?"

She didn't answer.

"D'you sit in here all the day? Don't you even go in for dinner? I do. Best part of school, dinner."

He sauntered out. Nasim pushed her book into her carrier bag and followed him to the dining-room, keeping a safe distance away from him. He knew she was behind him and walked along jauntily, hands in pockets, whistling. She watched him take a tray and cutlery and she joined the queue behind him. The room stank of cabbage and gravy and was noisy with the shrieking of chairs being pushed back and loud spurts of laughter between tables. She gazed round her. Most of the faces were white, though some were very black and one or two had the sallow skins of the far east. Everyone seemed to know each other, and to enjoy being together.

"What d'you want on it, love?" The dinner lady was speaking to her. Nasim looked down at the plate of meat in front of her.

"Is it halal meat, please?" she asked.

"Never heard of that, love," the dinner lady laughed. "It's good mutton, that."

"If not halal meat I can't eat."

"Suit yourself. Get a clean plate then. Potato? Cabbage?"

Nasim carried her plate to an empty table and sat down. Now that she had some dinner she didn't really want it, but at least she'd found out what everyone did at dinner time. That was progress, she supposed. For some reason she couldn't get out of her thoughts the meat man at the market where she and her mother and aunties shopped of a morning in Pakistan. He would sit crosslegged and barefoot on a board with his joints of meat round him and a paper to swat the flies away, and the old purdah women would come in their swathes of clothing and shout at him because his prices were too high, and her grandmother would laugh and ask him how much he wanted for his feet, they looked fresher than the meat.

Twagger was sitting at the next table to her. "Oi!" he called. "Didn't you want your meat?"

"Only killing halal way," she whispered, to herself rather than to him; to her plate of wet cabbage.

"I'll have it next time," he told her. He wiped his hand across his mouth and ran out of the cafeteria. He felt better now he'd eaten. It was a clear, cold afternoon, and he knew where he wanted to spend it.

Chapter Six

By the time Twagger got home that afternoon it was dark. He let himself in and went into the room. The television was on, and his father was asleep, snoring loudly, with some empty beer cans on the carpet beside him. Twagger knelt down and quietly picked up the cans. He drained one down the sink and kicked the empties under the kitchen table. His father woke up.

"What d'you do that for?"

"What for?"

"Wake me up for?"

"It's only early, Dad. Want a cuppa tea?"

"Aye, go on then." His dad stretched and wandered into the kitchen. He swilled his face under the cold water tap and dabbed it dry on a grey tea-towel. "What you been doing all day then?"

"School."

"Oh, aye!"

"Have! Did drawing this affie. Look."

He unrolled a scroll of paper from his pocket and held it up for his dad to look at.

"What's that supposed to look like?"

"It's a duck."

His father laughed. "Fat lot of good drawing ducks'll do you. Drawing dole, that's what you'll be drawing. Like your old man." He went back into the room with his cup of tea and flicked the television to another station. "They can keep their daytime telly!" he shouted. "Load of rubbish!"

Twagger looked round the mess in the kitchen: last night's pots still piled in the sink, unfinished cups of tea on the draining-board, a cornflakes box tipped on its side on the floor and spilling out its contents.

"Get us some fags from the off-licence, will you?" His father called. "And a couple more cans."

"You get them, Dad." Twagger suggested. "Do you good to get five minutes fresh air."

"Come here and say that," his father was half-joking, still in a good mood. Twagger went through into the room. "Honest, Dad," he said. "I wish you wouldn't drink."

"Doesn't do you any harm, does it?" his dad laughed. "Or do you get a hang-over from the fumes?"

"It chased my mum away, for a start," Twagger said quietly.

"You what?"

Twagger stepped back neatly from the swipe of his father's arm. "I mean it, though. She couldn't stand you drinking like that."

"Don't make me laugh." His father stood up unsteadily, and Twagger took another step back. "She cleared off because they shut the pit. It's their fault she cleared off. Couldn't live off my dole money. Too many high ideas, your mother."

"You don't have to blame them," Twagger shouted. "They didn't tell you to come home and spend all your dole money on beer and knock her about! Fancy hitting a woman. I'm glad she went, if you must know. I couldn't stand the sight of you hitting her."

He dodged his head back as his father's arm came across at him and then he ducked under and sprang round to the other side of the settee.

"Give us the money and I'll go for your fags, then," he said. His dad dug his hand into his pocket and brought out a handful of coins. "Just the fags, mind." He slipped past him and down the hall to the front door. "And I hope they choke you."

His dad sank back on to the settee and sat with his head in his hands while 'the programmes for very young children flickered brightly on his television screen.

Twagger ran up the street to the off-licence at the corner. Old Mrs Heaton was standing at her window when he went past, trying to pull the curtains across to keep out some of the draught and all the loneliness of darkness. She could just make Twagger out as he ran head down into the cold.

"He ought to wrap himself up better, that lad," she thought. "There's not much of him as there is. Spit of his dad, though, for all that."

She walked painfully round to her street door to pull the local evening paper through. "Haven't had a visitor for seven

39

whole days," she thought. "Mustn't grumble." She lifted her face up as if she was trying to squeeze back the sudden wetness that troubled her eyes. "Caroline might come tomorrow. Might. She just might."

Caroline had gone straight to her room when she came home from school. She changed out of her uniform and dropped her blouse into the basket in the bathroom, then ran downstairs to do her piano practise.

"Can't you play something quieter?" her sister Tanya shouted. "I can't hear telly."

"No," shouted Caroline. "I've got my lesson tonight."

"I haven't heard you practise at all this week," her mother said. She stood in the doorway with the baby over her shoulder. "I'll be getting one of Mrs Peace's letters again – 'Does Caroline really want to continue her lessons ... she's such a sweet girl, but....'"

"I do want to carry on," said Caroline. "We get so much homework at this school, though."

"D'you still want to take your grade five, then?"

Caroline nodded. "I mightn't get it."

"You get it," her mother warned her. "It's not free, you know, and neither are these lessons. And your dad's not made of money."

"I don't mind dropping French horn, though," Caroline called as her mother closed the door.

"No chance," her mother shouted. "I want you to stay in that orchestra. You don't know how lucky you are."

"I can't fit it in any more," Caroline moaned. "Youth orchestra's always on Saturday afternoons. I'm supposed to be going with Susan while she has her ears pierced tomorrow. And what about Mrs Heaton? I might have to give her a miss. I'd never get her wheelchair out in this anyway." She rummaged through her music pile and brought out her favourite piece. It was a Chopin prelude, and she loved it because the low notes were so dark, and all the melody was in the left hand. It suited her mood. "And there's Sprat," she whispered. "He said he's going to do his geography project in the library tomorrow morning.

40

I thought I might do mine there, too."

Sprat let himself into his house soon after five. He'd done some shopping on the way home from school. He dropped a bag of mushrooms in the drive and had to go back out to pick them up. Next door's cat wound itself round his legs and, when he bent down to stroke it, lay with its back in the snow and its legs up in the air to have its belly tickled.

"Daft Moggy," Sprat laughed. "What if humans did that?" He lay down next to the cat and waved his arms and legs about, then heard the front door slam. "Oh, heck." He'd left the key on the hall table with the rest of the shopping. "It's your fault, Moggins," he told the cat.

He stood up and slapped the snow off himself. If he climbed through any of the windows it would set the burglar alarm off, because they were on a different system from the front door. The only person who had a spare key was the lady who came in to clean for them, and she lived in town somewhere. He'd have to wait in the garage till his dad came home, and that could be hours. He hadn't seen him before eight any night this week, some nights he'd been in bed when he got back. They usually communicated by notes. He nibbled a frosty mushroom and ploughed across the snowy lawn to the garage. It was locked.

"That's funny," he thought. "Dad usually leaves it open when he goes out."

He decided to squat down in the front porch. He peered through the bobbly glass on the front door. He could see the pile of shopping on the hall table, and could just about make out the red and white plastic football on the end of his keyring. There was a light on in the kitchen, that he must have left on that morning. It wasn't unusual. He slid his back down the glass and nibbled another mushroom. He didn't like them much, but they'd been on the shopping list his dad had left out that morning. The door slowly opened behind him, and he slipped back with it till he was lying on his back on the hall carpet.

"Hiya." His dad grinned down at him.

41

"What are you doing here?" asked Sprat.

"I live here. Come and meet the budgie."

"How come you're home so early?" Sprat jumped up, spilling the rest of the mushrooms and squelching one into the doormat.

"I took the afternoon off," his dad said. "I've hardly seen you all week. I thought, I'll go home to my little six-foot sprat and for once we'll have a meal together. Home cooking! And then we'll go out to the pictures. What d'you think?"

"Hey, great Dad." Sprat scooped up the rest of the shopping and followed him into the kitchen. "Why did you lock me out then?"

"Anyone who rolls about in the snow with his feet in the air deserves to be locked out. Or locked up. Oi!"

He ducked away from the volley of mushrooms and sent them pelting back. In the lounge, the budgie cocked its head to listen to the laughter and cackled in response.

After school Nasim had gone straight to the little red-brick mosque where the muslims met for prayers. It was Friday, the main day of prayer, and though usually it was only the men and boys who went to the mosque, leaving the women to pray at home, her uncle wanted her to come to meet the Imam. She slipped her shoes off inside the door and waited for him. It was his home. He lived downstairs and upstairs he led the prayers in the room facing the holy place, Mecca.

He was very busy sorting out some problems with a young Asian family when she arrived. He wore a spotless white tunic and trouser outfit, his shalwar-kameeze, and was very like the Imam she knew at home. When he came to her at last they only had a few minutes to spend together before the sunset prayer. Men were already arriving and lining up their shoes next to Nasim's.

"Are you happy at your school?" he asked her in urdu.

"Yes, thank you," she said. "I wish there were other Asian girls in my class, though. I would make friends then."

"It's a pity your English is so good," he told her. "We could have sent you to the language centre first, and you'd have soon made friends. But don't wait for the English girls to talk to you,

Nasim. You must make an effort yourself. Are they unkind to you?"

"Oh no. Not unkind. They just don't talk. The only one who talks to me is a boy, and I mustn't talk to him."

He motioned to her to sit down with him on the floor. They were in the little room that the children used every night for their Qur'an lessons.

"Who says you mustn't, Nasim?"

"My brother."

"Your brother here or your brother in Pakistan?"

"My big brother in Pakistan. Tahir."

The Iman sighed. He came across this problem all the time. "Your brother is right," he said at last. "If you are in Pakistan. But you are in England, and you must do here what the western culture tells you to do. You may speak to a boy in your class at school. You are expected here to talk to boys, and you can do it. You are a good girl, Nasim. It is possible to be a Muslim girl and still take part in English life, and you must do that. Do you hope to stay here?"

"My brother doesn't want me to stay too long."

"Well," said the Imam. "He is your brother, and takes your father's place. But I would like you to stay. This is a good country."

"That is what my uncle Assan says. That's why he paid for Majad to come here, and then me. He says there is more opportunity for us in the West. Our country is so poor."

"Majad has been here a long time now, hasn't he? Three years?"

"Yes. He came when he was sixteen. Before my father died. He always wanted to live in England, so my uncle paid for him and now Majad helps him with his work. He loves it here."

Nasim wished privately that it was one of her sisters who was in England, instead. Two of her sisters were younger than Majad, even though they were married with babies. She missed them so much that her throat ached when she thought about them. There had been so much noise and laughter of women in her old home.

"I know Majad well." The Imam interrupted her thoughts.

"He is very proud of you, Nasim. He'll help you to settle down here."

Nasim nodded. There was no point in telling the Imam that Majad was even stricter with her than her big brother Tahir had been. It was all right for him to adopt Western ways and have English friends. "I never want to see you behaving like an English girl, d'you hear me?" he'd told her one day when they were out together, and she'd been smiling at the way some girls were throwing snowballs at a gang of older boys, shrieking with laughter. "And I never want to see you wearing English clothes, either. Father would never have allowed that."

The Imam stood up. "Time for prayer," he told her. "Go to the women, Nasim."

Nasim slipped away to kneel with her aunt Zarniga in the little room that was set aside for women to pray in. She thought of the pale mosque at home, glimmering in its canal reflection. She thought of her big house, and of lying out on the verandah on the straw charpoy beds and sharing the laughter and gossip of all her sisters and cousins. And she thought of her dearest friend, her great-grandmother Kauser, dancing for them at her sister's wedding party, swaying like a young girl in her cerise shalwar-kameeze, her bangles sparkling, her wide smile toothless, clapping her hands to the laughing women to bring them one by one into the dancing; bending over to Nasim, her favourite, to grasp her wrists in her dry soft hands and pull her up to join them.

"Not my baby now," she had laughed down to her. "My woman-sister."

Chapter Seven

Miss Peters had asked everyone to bring in something to talk about during the Wednesday English lesson. "Show and Tell", she called it. "Have you all brought your stuff then?" she asked as she walked in. "How about you, Martin? You've got some interesting-looking boxes there. Let's start with you."

Martin had been sitting biting his nails. When Miss Peters spoke to him he covered his mouth with his hand and turned round in his chair. "Can't," he muttered.

"Come on, Martin. It's not like you to be shy, goodness."

He wriggled his hand about and shook his head. Sprat, next to him, told him he was going red.

"Are you eating something?" Miss Peters asked. "Because if you are you can get rid of it."

Sprat pulled Martin's hand away from his face and stared at him. "He's a were-wolf!" He clutched his arms tight across his chest and banged his head on the desk top. "Look at him." His laughter howled in its top octave. "Were-wolf!"

"Let me see you, Martin."

Martin stood up and bared his teeth. A long slice of thumbnail was wedged between his two top front teeth so that his lip hung over the spike.

"Can't you get it out?" Miss Peters smiled.

Martin shook his head and sucked back the spittle.

"You shouldn't bite your nails," Donna told him. "It makes them go all frilly."

Martin wobbled the spike and sucked. "It'f ftuck, Miff."

Sprat howled again.

"Go outside and see what you can do," Miss Peters said. "Suck an icicle or something. And don't pull your teeth out."

She waited while Martin walked out, head down. "Who else is there?" she asked. "Simone, come on. What's in that box?"

Simone had brought a hamster, but as soon as she lifted it out of the box the girl next to her sneezed and she dropped it. It fell with its arms and legs splayed out like a bat, and then it scuttled away to freedom. Miss Peters casually sat on the edge of her desk and lifted her feet a couple of inches off the ground so it could pass freely underneath them. "You're worse than an infants' class," she told the red bobbing faces as hands and feet swung out in every direction to block the hamster's gallop. Nasim, bright-eyed with laughter, smiled up at her.

"Stay out!" Simone shouted as the door was pushed open. Mr Brown, grey-faced, stood in the doorway.

"Please close the door," Miss Peters begged him. "We've got an animal loose."

"An *animal* loose!" he repeated. He walked slowly to the front of the class while they stood in silence, listening for the furtive scamper. Stuart edged towards the door.

"Leave it!" Mr Brown shouted. He turned to Miss Peters. "I cannot believe what I am seeing. When I came across that yard I could not believe what I was hearing. Bedlam in here. Bedlam, Miss Peters."

"I can explain. . . ."

"And it's always bedlam in this class. Always. I think a class detention is called for. *Quiet!* Miss Peters is a young teacher – how many years have you been teaching, Miss Peters?"

"Two, but – "

"Two years. Is this the way to treat a young, inexperienced teacher? By taking advantage of her? By shouting your heads off and having animals running all over the place? Is it?"

The class shook their heads. Donna giggled silently and hysterically into her handkerchief.

"I see Martin Turner has been sent out for bad behaviour already," Mr Brown went on.

"No, he ... he got a thumb-nail stuck between his teeth," Miss Peters began bravely. She caught Donna's eyes and pleaded with her to stop snorting.

"This is an English lesson, I take it? Not circus skills or animal training or even dentistry?"

Miss Peters managed to straighten her face as he turned to her again. "It's an oral English lesson," she said. "Though we've lost our subject now you've left the door open. And we're ready to continue, if you don't mind, Mr Brown."

Sprat gave her a thumbs-up sign.

"I came in to look for Michael Sanders. Send him across if he deigns to turn up." Mr Brown strode out of the room abruptly and slammed the door to.

Miss Peters raised her eyebrows. "I'm sorry, Simone," she said. "We'll never find it out there."

"Can I go and look, though?"

"You and Helen. Five minutes."

Martin came back in as the girls went out. "Have you seen a hamster?" they asked him.

"I saw a big brown toad," he said. "He's just flopped off to main school."

"Now then Martin, have you sorted yourself out?" Miss Peters asked. "Because if you have, I'd like to get this lesson under way, and if you haven't, I'm going to abandon it and have a debate instead."

Martin came up to the front of the class carrying a black box about the size of a shoe box, and set it down on Miss Peter's table.

"I hope it's nothing alive," she said. "I really prefer dead things at the moment."

Martin laughed. "You might be sorry you said that, Miss." He lowered his bag onto the floor and opened the box. Inside was a shining black pistol. Everyone looked on in silence as he lifted it out. It had the numbers .177 painted on its sleek barrel. He turned it over in his hands, as gently as if it *was* an animal of some sort.

"Well," said Miss Peters quietly. "And what d'you do with that, Martin?"

"Miss, he robs banks!" Sprat said.

"Let Martin tell us," said Miss Peters. "I'll tell you something, Martin. I've never seen a gun before. Not a real gun. I find it very frightening and threatening, don't you, everyone?"

"How powerful is it?" asked Matthew. It wasn't like him to speak up in lessons. He was a quiet, tense boy. He had the long delicate fingers of a musician, and was very softly spoken. When the class were in their jokey moods he rarely joined in, but sat quietly and nervously smiling, not sullenly detached as Twagger always was, but as an outsider, observing. He had asked the

47

question everyone wanted to ask. Most of the class were quietened and alarmed by this gun; fascinated too, in an uncomfortable way.

"Well, it's not very powerful at all," said Martin. "I only use it indoors. It's only got a range of about five yards. But it could still cause a lot of damage."

"How can you use it indoors, though?"

"I've got this kind of mock shooting range set up in my bedroom. It's got this kind of extension thing on the end and I put corks in and shoot at models and that. Or you can put darts in. I've got this picture of a cat on my wall and I shoot darts at that."

"I think that's really horrible," said Donna. "Playing at being macho. You must be mental or something."

"When my dad uses it at the club he loads it properly, of course."

"It's not loaded now, though, is it?" asked Matthew.

"I hope not!" said Miss Peters, worried. "It's not, is it, Martin?"

He shook his head. "I'm not that daft, Miss."

While Martin was explaining about aiming his pistol, Simone and Helen came back in, red-cheeked with the cold and fed up because they hadn't found the hamster. Soon afterwards Twagger slipped in and huddled next to the radiator by his desk. He looked pale and tired, and the skin under his eyes was smudged like dark stains. He sucked his fingers while he watched Martin. Miss Peters decided to let him warm up before she sent him over to Mr Brown. At least he was in school; that was all that mattered for the moment.

"And what else have you brought, Martin? What's in the other box?"

Martin lifted the longer, thinner box out of his school bag and opened it carefully. "It's a .22 rifle, Miss."

He held it up for everyone to see. You could tell he was nervous with the effect his guns were having on the class.

"What do you use that for, Mart?" asked Sprat.

"I go with my dad," said Martin. "Hunting."

"Hunting what?"

"Rabbits and birds, mostly."

"That's really cruel," said Simone. "You mean you'd kill a live animal with one of these things?"

"Yes," said Martin. "I know, it is a bit cruel, but it's a sport, you see. You don't think about it being an animal, you just think about it being something moving for you to aim at."

"What if my hamster was running round now, there, now, running about on the floor like it was before? Would you shoot that, Martin? It's only about three inches long. would you? How could you kill something like that?"

"I knew I shouldn't have brought them, Miss," said Martin.

"No, no, this is interesting, Martin. Come on, speak up for yourself. Tell us why you like shooting as a sport."

"Miss, it's a skill. You have to be very steady and level, and not let anything distract you. Miss, I don't shoot animals. I only go with my dad to watch."

"What does he do with them when he's shot them?" asked Matthew.

"We eat them," said Martin. "It's no worse than you eating something that someone else has killed."

"I couldn't eat anything that's been killed," Simone shuddered. "We don't need to eat animals these days."

"Miss," said Nasim. "Please I say now?" It was the first time Nasim had offered to say anything in class. Miss Peters smiled at her to encourage her. Nasim stood up nervously and hung her head.

"In my home ..." she began.

"Speak up Nasim. I'd like everyone to hear you."

"In my home, nobody eat anything made of animal fat. Forbidden."

Twagger leaned over to her. "Tell them about that funny meat you eat. That kalal stuff."

"It spoke!" Stuart said. Miss Peters shook her head at him.

"Go on, Nasim. I'm interested."

"It is calling halal meat. It is because when it is slock ... slock ..."

"Slaughtered?"

"Yes, Miss. All the blood must be let out of it first."

49

"Yuck!" said Simone.

"She can't eat our meat," Twagger told them.

"No, miss. In school I must only have vegables."

"Vegables!" Susan snorted. "Vebbagles. Vlebbiges!"

"Quiet!" snapped Miss Peters. "Vegetables, Nasim."

"Yes, Miss. Vebbles. Vebbles."

Bubbles of laughter broke out again. Nasim smiled round at them.

Miss Peters clapped her hands. "Thank you, 3B. That's enough. Nasim has enough to put up with, coping with a new language, without having to try to understand why you're so rudely laughing at her. I think you've started some very interesting ideas, Martin, by bringing your guns in, and I'd like to continue to discuss some of these issues another day. We'll talk about blood sports next Wednesday, and whether it's right to eat animals, and ..."

"Miss, I don't think anyone should be allowed to buy a gun, Miss. They're too dangerous. . . ." Matthew stood up to speak, his hands clasped together as if he was praying.

"Good, Matthew. We'll discuss that too. All think what you'd like to say about these topics and we'll try to discuss them calmly without having a shouting match. Now sit down, Martin. Who else has brought something to do with their hobby?"

Twagger's hand shot up. "Miss ..."

Miss Peters looked surprised. "Wonderful, Michael. Come on then. Tell us what your hobby is."

"I don't like hobbies, Miss." He said. "Can I look at Martin's guns, though? Can I hold them, Miss?"

Before Miss Peters could speak the guns were being passed down the rows; boys clustered round Twagger's desk, whistling as they felt the weight of the guns, cradling them as though they were fragile, their faces tautening as they crooked fingers round the trigger. Twagger was in the middle of them, laughing up at them, his eyes sparkling with excitement.

"Come on, give them here," said Martin as the bell went. "Stop mucking about with them."

"Thank you for bringing them, Martin. We've had a really

interesting lesson," said Miss Peters. "And thank you, Simone. I'm so sorry about your hamster."

"So am I," said Simone. "I'll kill that Mr Brown."

"That's strong talk for a vegetarian," smiled Miss Peters. "But I think I know how you feel."

"Miss," said Caroline. "I feel as if something really awful is going to happen now. I wish Martin had never brought those things."

"Off you go," said Miss Peters, laughing at her. "We've had a lot of excitement during this lesson, that's what's worrying you. You're not used to being interested."

"Miss!" But Miss Peters laughed again and propelled her towards the door. "Off you go to Games," she said. "And have a good run round the hockey pitch. That'll get it out of your system. It's called adrenalin!"

Caroline swung her bag on to her shoulders and put her hand in for her gloves. She shouted and dropped the bag.

"What's up now?" asked Miss Peters.

"Simone's hamster! It's in my bag! Look at that – it's chewed up my art homework. Honestly Simone, my heart nearly popped out of my mouth when I touched it then!"

Simone brought the cardboard carton over and gently lifted her hamster into it. "I'll still kill him!" she said.

On her way to the staff room Miss Peters caught sight of Mr Bead going down the stairs to the changing rooms, and ran to catch up with him.

"Joe," she called. "Wait!"

Mr Bead glanced up and down the corridor then bent down to give her a quick kiss. "Haven't seen you for hours!" he said. "What are you looking so pleased about?"

"You!" she said. "And I've just had a fabulous lesson with Three Bead."

"They're a lovely class," he agreed. "I get on well with them too. Load of clowns half the time."

"Ah, but wait till I tell you. That lad they call Twagger spoke up three times. Three times, Joe. And he's gone off down to games with all the other lads, pleased as punch with himself."

"Great," said Mr Bead. "I've really been working on those

kids to be nice to him. I'm just off to find him now, as a matter of fact."

"Something else," said Miss Peters. "Nasim talked! They laughed at her, but she still talked. And little quiet Matthew."

"That's great, Liz. Tell me about it at lunchtime will you? I must catch them before they go out. I'll buy you a cheese sarnie at the pub!"

"But I do book club on Wednesdays," she called, as he pushed open the doors of the boys' changing-room. The racket in there drowned out her voice. "Never mind," she said out loud. "I'll cancel the book club. Blow it!" And she whistled jauntily all the way up to her lesson with the fifth form.

The last boy was just charging out of the room as Mr Bead went in. Stan Murphy, the games teacher, was about to lock the door.

"Stan!" Mr Bead called. "Can I have a quick word?"

"Not much time, Joe," the games teacher said. "They'll be up the trees if I don't keep an eye on them. What's up?"

"I was just wondering about Michael Sanders. I just wanted a word with you about him."

"Sanders? Never seen the lad. Always twags off games. I've given up chasing him."

"Didn't you see him today? I've just seen Liz – she said he came down here with the other lads."

"Didn't notice him, Joe. Mind you, I've had a lot of stuff to see to today – and two of the lads didn't want to go out at all. I know it's cold out there but I'll soon steam them up. I'll have to go."

"Hang on, Stan. It's important."

The games teacher leaned out of the outside door and blew a warning blast on his whistle. "Oi! Stand there and wait, you lot! No messing!" he yelled. He stuck his head back into the changing-room. "Right, Joe. What?"

"Have a look at Michael when they come back in. Don't make it obvious. I want to know if he's got any bruises on him. Will you do that?"

The games teacher nodded, puzzled, and ran off outside,

blowing his whistle to get the lads on to the field. Mr Bead took a quick look round the changing-room and went off to the staff room to get some marking done. And as soon as he'd closed the door, Twagger slid out from behind the lockers where he'd been hiding for the last ten minutes.

The last lesson before lunch was Geography. The girls were in the classroom first. The boys were all late, and when they did come it was in twos and threes, and they could be heard arguing with each other excitedly as they crossed over from the main building to the mobile. Mr Bead had set up a test for them, and as they came in he signalled to them to go quietly to their seats and get on with their work. Soon all the boys were back except Martin and Twagger. Everyone was restless, twisting round to look out of the window to see if either of them were coming. It was almost time for the bell when Martin came in at last. He was out of breath, as if he'd been running all round the school. He burst into the room, looked quickly round for someone, and was about to run out again when Mr Bead called him back.

"What've you been doing all this time, Martin?"

"Sir," said Martin. "Someone's nicked my guns."

Chapter Eight

The pub opposite the school was usually quiet at lunch-times. It made a change from the shrill clatter of the school canteen or the light banter that usually went on in the staff-room.

Liz Peters sat alone in the lounge bar waiting for Joe Bead to turn up. She decided to have one more Britvic and then go back to catch up on her marking. She felt self-conscious sitting on her own, especially when she'd finished reading the *Guardian*.

Even if he did turn up at last she didn't want to see him. She didn't really want him to know that she'd sat there on her own for half an hour waiting for him. She'd just decided to do without the drink when he came in, breathless, talking to himself as usual, pulling coins out of his pocket and scattering them on the pub carpet. She smiled and sat down again. "Joe! Over here!"

He waved and mimed a drink and she nodded. He pushed his way to the bar, ordered the drinks and came back carrying a pint of beer and a glass of orange and with a packet of crisps dangling from his teeth.

"Tate zen," he said. She took the packet and one of the glasses from him and made room for him on the plush bench beside her. "Sorry, love," he said. "Sorry I'm late."

"What was it this time?"

"Have a guess."

She opened the crisp packet and handed him one. "Twagger?"

"Got it in one."

"Joe. Why d'you spend so much time on that lad?"

"Because he's worth it."

"Michael Sanders? He's never here."

"Exactly." He pushed his chair back and went to the bar again, and came back with two cheese sandwiches. He ate his without saying anything, deep in thought.

"You're miles away," Liz said softly. "Tell me what he's done now."

"I don't know if he's done anything. But Martin's guns have

54

gone missing, and so has he."

"They haven't!"

"They're not loaded, of course. It's not that dramatic."

"So why's he taken them?"

"Why? I don't know. I could make a guess."

"To threaten his dad with."

"Wouldn't surprise me."

"Or worse."

"Don't be daft, Liz. He's only a kid."

She shuddered. "I keep thinking about that awful piece of writing he did for me the other day. Nasty, horrible, sadistic...."

"He was getting it out of his system. It probably did him good."

"Didn't do me much good. It really upset me. I think there must be a lot of violence in him, to write like that."

"He sees a lot of violence, Liz."

"Violence breeds violence. That's what they say."

"Anyway. These guns. I don't know what to do about all this."

"Tell the boss."

"What good would that do? What on earth would that do?"

"It would take some of the responsibility off your shoulders. Stop taking it all on yourself, Joe. He's nothing to do with you."

"He's everything to do with me."

Liz looked round anxiously. Joe was shouting. She finished her sandwich slowly and dipped up the crumbs on her finger-nail. "Why?"

"Because I like the kid." Even as he said it he could see Twagger slouching alone across the field to his street, bag slung over his shoulder, always alone. "I don't think he's got one friend in this school."

"There's lots of kids like that."

"I don't know, Liz, we've got a lot to answer for, teachers. We lump a load of kids together in a room and we keep them there for hours on end and we expect them to do all kinds of things. Don't we, though? We never stop to think what's really going on in their heads, what's happened to them at home that morning and what they're going to have to face when they get home at night. We carry on as if school is the only thing that mattered. It's the thing that matters least."

"With some kids," said Liz, "if they didn't have school, they wouldn't have anything." She looked at her watch. "Come on, Joe. Time we were earning our living."

Joe Bead was surprised to see Twagger at his desk for registration that afternoon. "Where were you last lesson, Michael?" he asked him.

Twagger shrugged, half-turned, gazing out of the window.

"You missed Games, and you missed Geography. You can't just turn up when you feel like it, you know. You can't just turn up to register and then go home again."

"Don't go home," Twagger muttered.

"No," said Mr Bead quietly. "I don't suppose you do. Where do you get to, Michael?"

Just then Martin came in, red-faced and breathless from running round the school. He ignored Mr Bead and went straight to Twagger's desk.

"What've you done with them?" he shouted.

"What have I done with what?" said Twagger, pushing back his chair, mock-scared.

"Sit down, Martin," said Mr Bead.

Martin ignored him. "You know what I'm talking about. Give them back, Twagger. I'll get done if I don't take them home tonight. I'll never be able to use them again."

Twagger smiled. "Don't know what you're on about."

"Tell him, Sir, tell him," pleaded Martin. "It's my dad's club night tonight. I've had it if he finds out...."

"I thought they were your guns."

"No, Sir. They're my dad's. I'm not old enough to have a licence for them yet."

"And you didn't ask him if you could bring them to school?" Martin went red.

"Martin. Were you telling the truth when you said the guns weren't loaded?"

"I don't know, Sir. I don't think they were loaded. My dad's

56

very careful about things like that."

"But you don't know for certain."

Martin had to clear his throat to answer. "No, Sir."

The class went ghostly quiet. Mr Bead was cold in the pit of his stomach. He tried not to look at Twagger.

"You'd better sit down, Martin."

"I can't, Sir. I'm in a right state about this."

"Sit down while I think."

Martin went to his desk and pulled his chair back. He sat with his head buried in his folded arms, slumped across the desk. Sprat whispered to him, "I'll help you find them, Mart."

Everyone watched Mr Bead. He came up to Twagger's desk at last and pressed his hands down flat on the surface, leaning down so Twagger couldn't avoid his eyes.

"Where are they, Michael?"

Twagger tipped his chair back and laughed up at him, but his eyes were scared. "Why me? What've I done?"

"Never mind why. Where?"

"I'll get you, Twagger," said Sprat.

"Where are they, Michael?"

Twagger grinned up at Mr Bead, mocking his low, quiet voice. "Don't ask me. Ask Matthew."

"Don't be ridiculous," snapped Mr Bead.

"Matthew is a naughty boy who wanted Martin's little toy. Teacher give his bum a smack. Teacher make him bring it back," giggled Twagger, in a high child's voice this time.

"He's going mad," thought Mr Bead. "So am I. Mad." He swung away from Twagger towards Matthew's chair. It was empty.

"The birdie's flown," said Twagger. "Quack quack quack."

"Has anyone seen Matthew?" Mr Bead asked calmly. His heart felt like a bird, beating rapidly and insistently up towards his throat.

"Stuart, have you seen Matthew?"

"No, Sir," said Stuart, puzzled. "He asked to be excused during games, Sir."

"And you haven't seen him since?"

"No."

"Has anyone seen Matthew?"

Silence. Mr Bead turned back to Twagger. The boy was laughing up at him, white-faced and pale-eyed. He felt like shaking him.

"Do you know where he is?"

"I know where he was, and that was where he shouldn't have been."

"Michael; *Where is Matthew?*"

Twagger's smile stuck.

"That'd be telling, Sir. Nice boys don't tell tales."

The bell went for the end of registration. No one moved. Another class swarmed up to the door, knocking on the windows and leering through. Mr Brown rattled the door handle and then pushed his way in. "Taken root, have we?"

"You'd better go, class," said Mr Bead, weary. "Martin, Michael ... you stay. You'd better come and see the Head with me."

"Trouble?" Mr Brown gave him his thin smile. "Thought this was your class of angels, Mr Bead."

Joe Bead didn't bother to answer him. The class trooped out. He waited for Twagger and Martin to pack their bags up and they trailed behind him, Twagger automatically glancing down the corridor to see where he could escape to.

The Headmaster's door was shut, and the "Wait" light was on. He didn't answer Mr Bead's knock.

"We'd better wait," said Mr Bead. "What's your next lesson?"

"Drawing," said Twagger.

"Liar," said Martin. "It's French."

Twagger shrugged. "I'm doing drawing."

They waited ten minutes before the door opened. Matthew walked out, white-faced. He brushed past Mr Bead and ran off down the corridor. The Head's "enter" light flicked on. "Come on, lads," said Mr Bead, and pushed them in in front of him. Lying across the Headmaster's desk were Martin's guns.

"How did they get there, then?" asked Liz, later that evening. She and Joe Bead were eating curried lentils and pitta bread

58

in her ferny flat.

"The caretaker's wife found a fifth year with them. He frightened the life out of her, apparently."

"I'm not surprised," said Liz. "Half of them frighten the life out of me just by looking at me."

"Well, she had the sense to haul him off to the Head, and this lad said he'd found the guns in a bin! Dumped in the bins round the back of the kitchens!"

"Anyone could have found them."

"Exactly. Anyone did. This lad swore he'd found them there, and then Mrs Mulloney said she'd seen one of the third year lads sneaking round there at dinner-time, and one of the dinner ladies said it was Matthew, because she gives him meat scraps for his dog, apparently."

"And was it?"

"He admitted it. He'd taken it into his head to relieve Martin of his guns because, believe it or not, he thinks they're dangerous. He dumps them in a school bin for anyone to find because he thinks they're dangerous!"

Liz cleared away the plates. "It's me that's dangerous. That's the last time I'll have a trendy lesson with that lot. They can do comprehensions every day from now on."

Joe laughed. He followed her into the kitchen and filled up the sink.

"I don't mean it," she went on. "I'm not that much of a masochist. I can't stand marking comprehensions. I can't even do the things myself, they're so boring."

"The worst thing that's come out of this," said Joe, "is the fact that I was convinced that Twagger had taken the things. What's more, I accused him of taking them. And he knew I thought he'd done it, and he was laughing at me. I've tried all term to help that kid, and now I've undone everything. I'm back where I started with him. Further back. I hated him, when he was laughing at me in the classroom. I could have hit him. And he knows it."

"It's not the worst thing," said Liz. "The worst thing is that we both know that Twagger could have taken the guns. And what if he had, Joe? What then?"

59

Chapter Nine

Every week Nasim sat alone in the girls' changing rooms during indoor games. One day in late February she was joined by Susan. Nasim just knew her as one of the live-wires of the class, very talkative, one of Caroline's gang.

"Hiya," Susan said to Nasim, pleased to have someone to talk to.

"Hello." Nasim, shy, looked up and lowered her eyes again.

"I'm not doing games today," Susan said. "I've got a bad stomach."

"I'm sorry."

"You never do games, do you?" said Susan. "Don't you like them?"

"I can not," said Nasim.

"Course you can. You'll soon learn them. We'll be doing hockey soon, when the field dries out. Can't wait. You can get your teeth knocked in, of course, but you don't have to think about that."

"Teacher say me not play. My brother say me not play."

"Why?"

"Majad say me not to wear games clothes. Teacher say me I can not playing without games clothes," she said simply, staring at the floor.

"You'd look pretty daft running round a hockey pitch in those baggy things."

"They my pyjamas."

Susan giggled. "Pyjamas! Bit posh for pyjamas! Why can't you wear shorts?"

"It ... it my religion."

Susan nodded. She didn't really understand.

"I must wear my pyjamas. Now teacher say me I must wear tracksuit trows, but I have not got some."

"You'd better get some, then, Nasim. You can't stay out of things for ever."

She wandered round the changing room, bored. "Want some chewy?"

"No, thank you."

"I suppose that's against your religion as well."

Nasim said nothing.

Susan flopped back on to the bench opposite her.

"You're going to have to try to be more English, Nasim."

"I am English," said Nasim quietly. "I born here."

"Here?"

"Yes. Here. Not far away here. My mother father go back to Pakistan when I am baby."

"You're kidding!" Susan blew a bubble slowly and let it flatten against her lips. "Guess where I was born? Hong Kong! It's true! My dad was in the Air Force there. You're probably more English than I am!"

There was a roar on the playing-fields, where the boys were doing outside games in spite of the sodden pitch. Susan climbed on the central-heating pipes and tried to look through the windows, but they were too high. She walked along the pipes, balancing herself with her hands against the wall, till she fell off. She came back to the bench opposite Nasim.

"Why did you come back to England?"

"My brother here. My uncle and auntie. They ask me to come."

"And where are your parents?"

"My mother stay at home with my nanny-ma Kauser. She very, very old. And my big brother Tahir and his family. Many, many family."

"What about your dad?"

"My father dead." Nasim's voice was quiet and steady. "In the summer he die."

"Did your mum want you to come?"

Nasim shook her head. "My mother cry and cry. But my Uncle Assan want to look after me like my father, they very close brothers. My father would wish to do the same for him. And she knows that Majad is happy in England with him. Also my teacher say I will do very well in an English school, very lucky to have this chance."

Susan laughed. "Lucky! It's a right dump, this place!"

"You don't like? It very lovely after my little school. No

dusty floors, no insects. Many books. I can work here better."

"So did you want to come to England?"

"I must do as my family say," said Nasim simply. "That is our custom. Both my brothers very strict Muslim. Tahir makes Majad promise that I will not lose my Muslim culture here. My uncle aunt want me to settle here like them. My mother just want me to be happy. I come because she think it best for me."

Susan stared at her. She couldn't imagine having to go away from her own mother to a foreign country. "Well," she said at last. "So what do you think of it round here?"

"Round here very nice," said Nasim.

"But not as nice as Pakistan?"

"No. Nothing as nice as Pakistan. It my country, you see."

"D'you want to come out and watch the lads play, Nasim?" Susan broke the sad silence at last. "It's a right laugh. You should see them skidding about in the mud and the snow – they just don't care how mucky they get. They like it!"

Nasim shook her head, and Susan slipped her coat over her shoulders and wandered outside.

In the girls' changing room the hum of the radiators was louder even than the shouts coming in from the field. It was a comforting sort of hum, almost like the low, steady voice of a woman singing. Nasim closed her eyes. She had a letter from Tahir in her pocket; it told her that they loved her and missed her and that he only wanted her to be happy. It also told her that her old great-grandmother was ill in hospital. How the old woman would hate that! When Nasim's father had been ill and dying in hospital the women of the house had gone to his ward every day to feed and wash him; Nasim had gone too, and she and her great-grandmother would walk up and down the ward to talk to the other families gathered round the beds. The wards were crowded and too hot and dark, and noisy with groans and wailings and chatter and laughter. "Tck! Tck!" the old woman had said. "What a place to die! I would rather die out in the streets with all the poor beggars. At least I would see the sunshine and the stars there."

When the bell rang for the end of school, Nasim put her winter coat on and went home alone, as usual. The house was warm and sweet-smelling with spices; cinnamon and ginger. Nasim hung her coat and bag in the hall next to the picture that she had brought from home for her aunt and uncle. It had a geometric pattern round the border, and in the centre were words from the holy book, the Qur'an. She traced the words now with the tip of her finger, repeating them quietly to herself, and then she went into the kitchen to help her aunt get the meal ready. Her brother and uncle would be at work or maybe the mosque for the sunset service. The two little ones were watching television.

"Today I have an English friend," Nasim said, smiling.

Her aunt laid out chillies for the girl to chop. "Good girl, Nasim." She spoke to her in Punjabi.

"Her name's Susan. She's very funny."

"You may ask her home, one day."

"Oh no," said Nasim quickly. "She's very nice. But she is not Asian."

Her aunt laughed. "Nasim, Majad would like you to work with him tomorrow morning. That is very good."

Nasim was horrified. "On the stall? Oh, Auntie, must I? What if any of the girls from school saw me?"

"What if they did?"

"They'd laugh at me."

"Why should they laugh at you because you're doing a good job of work? Your uncle must go to the warehouse on Saturday, and Majad must have help. It must be you."

"I'll do it then, but I'll hate it."

"It will be very good for your English."

Little Yasmine ran into the kitchen and helped herself to a green okra finger from the pile that Aunt Zarniga was trimming. She bit into it before it was snatched away from her.

"You don't speak English," Nasim reminded her aunt. "You never speak English, and it doesn't matter."

"That's because I never need to speak English," said her aunt. "Your Uncle Assan goes everywhere with me. He speaks for me. But you are a new girl. You have been allowed to learn to speak for yourself. It will help to make you happy here."

She scooped up the chopped chillies and held them under the cold water to wash them, then dropped them into a pan of crushed spices sizzling in ghee oil.

"There is a thing I wish to know," said Nasim slowly. "Are you happy here?"

It was a long time before her aunt spoke. "It is not a question to be answered," she said at last.

Next morning Nasim set out with Majad when it was still dark. The roads had frozen again during the night and were treacherous to walk on. A few cars went past them with their headlights full on. Nasim pulled the hood of her coat up and huddled into it. When they reached the market many of the stall-holders were already there, pulling the tarpaulins off their stalls or sitting on crates drinking tea from vacuum flasks, all their transistor radios playing music from the same station. Uncle Assan had a good stall of men's clothes: jumpers and socks and scarves. Nasim straightened out the displays and stroked the soft wool. She loved the feel of it. Some people were already buying from the fruit and vegetable stalls, standing in a patient, orderly queue.

"They're very polite here," Majad smiled. "You don't see them shoving each other and bartering like they do at home. Have a wander round, Nasim. We won't get any customers yet."

He settled himself on a crate inside the stall and took out his Open University books. He was studying law. Nasim went to look at the other neat stalls. They weren't anything like the bright, rickety market stalls she used to visit with her mother, with all their pungent smells and colour and clamour; chickens squawking round her feet, bins of rich golden saffron and earthy coriander and garam masala, floating silk dupattis, patterned red carpets, her aunts gossiping with their loud laughter in the sunshine.

She went back to her uncle's stall and stroked the dark materials again. Then she noticed a rack of sportswear. She lifted off some blue tracksuit trousers and went round into the back of the stall.

"Majad." She held out the trousers. "I want these."

He laughed. "You want menswear trousers?"

"I need them for school."

"No, Nasim," he said. "You can't have them for school."

"If you don't say yes," she said firmly. "I will put them in a bag and take them home. I must play girls' Games if I'm to be like the other girls."

He put down his books and studied her. He had never known her to speak back to him like this. Then he held the trousers against himself, laughed, and went outside. He came back with the smallest pair.

"Here," he said. "Maybe Aunt Zarniga will help to make them the right size for you. But never let me see you in things like that."

He picked up his books again and Nasim hugged the trousers to her chest. "Lovely, lovely," she sang in English. "Lovely, lovely tracksuit trows!"

By the end of the morning she could hardly flex her fingers, they were so cold. She watched people as they came to her stall; smiled at them as they fingered and ruffled the garments, took the money from the buyers and smiled at them as they went away again. After a while she was too tired to smile; she found it hard to keep concentrating in English. Majad did most of the selling, then, and just passed her the money to change. Her back and feet ached. She saw Caroline passing with one of the other girls from class, she didn't know her name. The other girl glanced at her when she passed and said something to Caroline that made her laugh, but when Caroline turned to look at Nasim she didn't seem to recognised her, and Nasim was glad of that.

"You have some food," Majad told her. "I'll watch the stall, and then we'll swap over."

She was thankful for the rest. She sank down on to the crate and pulled the food bag open. Her aunt had packed a little pot of yellow dahl for them, made from spiced lentils, and some fresh chapatti bread; and there was a flask of sweet, milky tea. Nasim had just finished eating when her uncle arrived.

"You can go home now," he told her. "Just watch the stall for a few minutes while Majad and I have some food, and then you can go."

Then two men took her place behind the stall, and Nasim, stiff now from sitting, picked up the bag her tracksuit trousers were in and moved round towards the front. It was then that she saw Twagger.

He was standing with his back to her at first, sideways on to the stall, his hand resting on the pile of jumpers. He glanced quickly round as if he was looking for someone, but the little serving space by the till was empty. She moved to it, shy that he would see her, ready to smile at him if he did look at her; and in that slow moment when all the market sounds seemed to distort and fade and come together again in their high, meaningless, cackling pitch, she watched his hand slide to pull down a green V-neck pullover from the stall, and roll it and push it so it was under his jacket. She watched his white face turn and lift and his pale eyes lock into hers, and saw mirrored there for an instant her own surprise and alarm and recognition. Then he darted away and was lost from sight among the Saturday shoppers.

Chapter Ten

By half-term the sides of the streets were still piled with grey snow. Nights were as cold as they'd ever been, and the temperature hardly crept above freezing in the daytime. Mrs Heaton hadn't been out of her house for weeks, and though she always greeted Caroline with a cheerful shout of hello when she came to see her, she spent her days by the window, staring out at the cold light.

Caroline's dad worried about his bees, and spent the early evenings bent up against his hives, listening out for humming. Nasim had never known such cold before. At night in bed she cuddled her small cousin Yasmine and told her about the distant, hot country that the little girl had never seen. "Already the winter will be over there. Your flowers will be growing, yellow jasmine. And pansies. One day I take you there," she promised. "And the sun shine nice, and people are friendly." It sounded like a fairy-tale.

Twagger stayed indoors through most of the cold. His father had a series of letters from school asking him to go and see Mr Brown or the Head. He thrust a fistful of them into Twagger's face one day.

"Why should I go trailing over there to see that lot? You tell me?"

Twagger shrugged. "I don't know what they're on about. I do go to school."

"So you're telling me they're all blind, is that it? Fine flamin' school that is, if all the teachers are walking round with white sticks. Don't make me laugh."

One afternoon they had a visit from the Education Welfare officer. Twagger was in his room when the man came, and his father called him down.

"Now. Tell the man why you won't go to school. Tell him it's not me that keeps you away from the place."

"Tell me, Michael," the man said. "We're all concerned about you, you know."

Twagger glanced up at the stranger, a half-smile playing

about his lips. "There's no need to be bothered about me. I can look after myself."

"Do you hate school? Is that what it is?"

Mr Sanders laughed at that. "My old man hated the army, but he had to do it, didn't he? I hated the pit, but I had to go down there, didn't I? Dead of night, off out in the rain, down in the cold. Like a holiday camp that was."

"Do you, Michael?"

Michael sat back in his chair and closed his eyes, smelling the soapy perfume of the shampoo he'd just used. He'd had a bath that morning and he was wearing his new green jumper for the first time, though it had been in his drawer for nearly a week. Even now, as he fiddled with a worm of wool dangling from one of the cuffs, he remembered the look in Nasim's eyes at the market. He'd avoided her all week, but once they had come face to face in the corridor. Usually she was the one to look away, but that time she'd looked at him steadily. Her brown eyes told him nothing, but they left him with a cold, uncomfortable feeling inside him that was quite new to him.

She was on her way to girls' Games, and she had unwrapped her tracksuit trousers in the changing room and put them on hurriedly, not allowing herself the moment of triumph she'd hoped for when she followed the white girls for the first time into the gym. She was ashamed of them, and she would always feel guilty now when she put them on, because she would always associate them with the day a boy stole from her kind uncle's stall and she allowed him to do it.

"Are you listening to me. Michael?"

Twagger nodded. He didn't like this man any more. He was bored with him; he didn't like the way the man stared at him, the way he smiled at him as if he was a friend, the way he tried to look comfortable on the ugly brown chair with the broken spring, as if he had a right to be there. Abruptly, Twagger stood up and ran upstairs. He crouched on the top step, hugging his arms round himself, listening.

"I'll give the boy till the end of next half-term to settle down," the man told Twagger's dad. "If it doesn't work, we'll have to think about making other arrangements for him."

"What kind of other arrangements?"

"A different sort of school, maybe."

"You're not sending him away," Mr Sanders said, alarmed suddenly. He switched off the television. "Leave him alone. Leave us both alone. There's only one thing wrong with that school he goes to – they're too soft with him. Give him a belting when he comes in late, that's what he needs. I should know. I'm the one who knows him. I'm his dad."

He thrust up his red face and shouted, with bubbles of spittle trickling from the corners of his lips. The black stubble on his chin rasped as he wiped the back of his hand across his mouth. "He's my kid." His voice broke to a whimper. "I can handle him."

The stranger watched Mr Sanders quietly, then he stood up, buttoning up his heavy winter coat, pulling the collar up round his ears, smoothing his soft leather gloves over his fingers. "Then we all want to do what's best for him. I'll see you again, Mr Sanders."

He let himself out.

Twagger wore his new jumper to school the next day, glad of its warmth. He came in while Mr Bead was doing the register, and the boys set up a wild jeer as he sat down. Mr Bead looked up and frowned. Sprat, like the conductor of an orchestra, stood up with his hands spread out and drew them swiftly apart, silencing them instantly. He grinned and bowed and sat down again.

"Perhaps I ought to remind you all," said Mr Bead quietly, not looking at the class but at Twagger, who was staring at his desk-top and nursing his arms as if they hurt him. "We're on half-term next week. So don't come in by mistake, will you?"

Twagger spent the whole day in school, and he didn't speak to a soul, or open a book, or lift his eyes from his desk. At the end of the day he slid his jacket on with difficulty, wincing as he tried to bend his arm, and stood up just as Nasim was passing his desk.

"Are you hurting?" she asked him.

He pushed away from her and walked, head-down, through

the slush of the field to his house.

After school Sprat and Caroline walked down to the Frenchgate Centre together. Caroline's mum had asked her to fetch home some vegetables for the evening meal.

"What are you having for tea?" she asked Sprat.

"Dunno. Take-away, usually, when Dad gets home. If he gets home."

"D'you get on all right with your dad?"

"He's O.K. He doesn't bother me."

Caroline nodded. She wanted to ask him if he still missed his mum.

"I don't see much of him," Sprat went on. "He's never in. He does a lot of travelling for his firm."

"Is there just you then, at home?"

"Most of the time. Yes."

She pictured Sprat making his own meal, sitting eating on his own in front of the television. Her house was always noisy with her younger sister and brothers, bouncing with their shouts.

"I can't imagine going home to an empty house," she said. "There's always someone in at ours."

"You get used to it."

"Do you like it, though?"

"Not much," he asked. "Why? Would you?"

"D'you want that cabbage, love?"

Caroline turned away and paid for the vegetables. She shoved them down into her schoolbag.

"You and Twagger have got something in common, then," she said.

"What's that supposed to mean?"

"Don't get mad at me, Sprat. You know what I mean."

"Me and Twagger've got nothing in common. My dad doesn't hit me."

He walked away in front of her, hands stuffed in his pockets. Caroline wondered what they'd say at home if she invited Sprat back for tea. She was always having friends round; her mum liked her to bring her friends home, as long as they were the sort who'd muck in and not be surprised at the untidy mess the house was always in. But she'd never taken a boy home before. She imagined her mother's raised eyebrows and her father's teasing smile, and her sister Tanya giggling behind the door. It would be awful. But she wanted Sprat to know she was sorry.

"D'you want to come to our house for tea? I'm sure they wouldn't mind."

"No, thanks," said Sprat. "I hate cabbage."

When Caroline had finished all her shopping they wandered round to the snack bar. Sprat brought a five-pound note out of his pocket to pay for the two milk-shakes. They sat on high stools at the counter.

"You're loaded," said Caroline.

He shrugged. "Dad's always giving me money. He leaves out fivers for me all the time, to get chips or a take-away or summat. Never asks for the change. I've got a drawer full of cash at home. Want some?" He spilled out a handful of cash across the counter. "Want it?" A sudden spurt of anger welled up in him. He pulled more coins out of his pocket, and more.

"Don't be daft, Sprat." Caroline was shocked. "Put it back. Please."

"Well. I don't want it." He scooped up a handful of the coins and fed them into the shute of a collecting box on the counter. "Some little orphan is going to be very happy. What good's money anyway? It only weighs your pockets down."

Caroline was uncomfortable. She didn't understand Sprat when he was in this sort of mood. She finished her milk-shake and slid down from her swively stool.

"Thanks for the milk-shake. I'll have to go."

He followed her out of the snack-bar. He felt fed up. The milk-shake had made him feel slightly sick. He didn't want to go back to his empty house yet. He felt awkward about leaving Caroline now. "Would your mother mind if I didn't eat the cabbage?" he asked.

Caroline hesitated. She thought of her sister again. "I think I'd better ask Mum first," she said. "I'll ask if you can come on Wednesday." Tanya went to Brownies on Wednesdays, and always had tea at a friend's house.

"Don't bother." Sprat was angry again, sorry for himself. Caroline watched him slouch away. No point following him; anyway, she didn't even like him when he was in this sort of mood.

Sprat walked round town for a bit before he went home. He went back at about six. The house was in darkness, as usual. He let himself in and went into the kitchen. He put some bread in the toaster and rooted round in the cupboard for something to put on it. The marmalade jar was empty. He ran his finger round inside it, licked it, and put the jar back in the cupboard. The toast popped up. He shook some tomato ketchup on to it and carried it, balanced on a carton of strawberry yoghurt, into the front room. He switched on the television, settled himself down to watch a quiz show, and saw the note propped up behind the clock on the mantelpiece.

"Another note, another fiver," he said to the budgie. "Get yourself a take-away, Sprat. I won't be home till late."

The budgie cackled and kissed its reflection.

Sprat waited till the quiz show was over to open the note. "I'll be home late," it said. "Get yourself a take-away, and clean up, please. Your mother rang. She's coming to see you tomorrow."

He felt a swell of nervousness spreading cold as snow inside him. He sat down on the edge of the chair, balancing his unfinished bread and ketchup on the back of his hand. "Clean up, please. Your mother rang. She's coming to see you tomorrow. Your mother. Tomorrow." He sat repeating and repeating it as though he was teaching the budgie to talk, understanding nothing of the words except that they made his eyes prickle and his throat ache and his stomach ice-cold.

A smiling woman on the television screen told him he should give his man Flora and he suddenly threw his piece of toast at her. It slid slowly down the screen, trailing a slime of ketchup like cold blood. He threw the chair cushion after it. He kicked over the coffee table, spilling the last of his fizzy orange juice and a stack of car magazines and Sunday colour supplements. He tipped his school bag on to the sprawling pile and kicked the hearthrug round it all. He jerked his arm along the mantelpiece, scooping off his school photograph, the clock, the ashtray that he'd made in his first attempt at pottery and that no one had ever used, the mottled shell from Malta, the Wedgewood vase, all splintered and smashed like sharp cries of pain on the tiled hearth. He couldn't stop himself. It wasn't him. It was a hot rage in his head and a cold quiet in his limbs, and it was a sick spread in the pit of his stomach.

He ran upstairs and grabbed the photograph from behind the goldfish bowl and ran downstairs with it again. He smeared it round and round the sticky television screen. A newsman told him about famine in Africa. A woman held a dying baby with arms like sticks to her flat breasts. He ripped up the photograph and scattered it like feathers, or snow, or ashes, round the room. Then he ran to Caroline's.

His father came home at about nine. He sat in his car in the drive for a bit, letting the long journey from Birmingham drain away from him, then let himself into the house.

"I'm home, Sprat!" he called. He picked up his post and ran upstairs. "I'll be down in a sec. Having a shower first." He kicked his shoes off in his bedroom and threw his tie on to the bed.

"Turn the telly down!" He listened for a moment at the top of the stairs, sighed, and ran downstairs to do it for himself. He stopped dead, taking in the mess on the floor and the hearth. The budgie pecked the bars of its cage, impatient for food. Sprat's dad stepped over the mess and switched off the television. He ran his finger down the screen and sniffed it, then, puzzled, crouched down to examine the stuff on the carpet. One by one he picked out the fragments of photograph, wiping the yoghurt and ketchup off them, arranging them like a jigsaw puzzle on the coffee table. He stared at them for a long time. They he swept them into the palm of his hand, tipped them into the waste paper basket, and slowly and carefully tidied up the room.

Caroline's younger sister opened the door to Sprat. She gazed at him solemnly.

"Can I see Caroline? Quick!"

She still gazed at him.

"Tanya? Who is it?" a woman called.

"Caroline's hunky boyfriend," said Tanya. "He's in a right state."

"Get her, will you," muttered Sprat. "Tell her it's Sprat."

"It's Sprout!" giggled Tanya. "Brussel Sprout!"

"Russell?" The woman came to the door. "Come in, Russell. She's just gone round to Heidi's for a few minutes. Come in and wait for her."

"No, thanks," said Sprat.

"Please," said Tanya.

"All right."

He stood awkwardly in the hall while Tanya smiled up at him and Caroline's mother came up and down the stairs getting the younger children ready for bed. She sat on the stairs chatting to him while she changed the baby's nappy, and he averted his eyes from the sticky ooze she was wiping up while he tried to answer her questions about school. Tanya settled herself on a chair and smiled at him. He smiled back, shocked at the smell coming from the baby's nappy next to his feet.

"I'm sorry about this, Russell," Caroline's mother said. "Have you got any babies in your house?"

"No," he said. "Not really."

"I see." The phone rang and she swung the baby over to Sprat. "Hold him a sec. would you?"

The baby sprawled a wet hand across Sprat's eye.

"Cooeee!" he murmured to it. "Cooee!"

"It's Caroline!" Mrs Shepherd called to him, smiling. "Caroline. Russell's here. He's waiting for you."

The baby belched a milky stream on to Sprat's shoulder. Tanya giggled.

"Course you do. No need to be coy about it, love, he's very nice!" Mrs Shepherd said to the telephone. She winked at Sprat. "She's trying to pretend she doesn't know anyone called Russell!"

"She doesn't," Sprat tried to explain. The baby started to cry. "It's not my name."

"Well, you said – "

"No, I didn't. You did. She did...." The baby opened its mouth in a huge, wet, loud fury, red-faced and damp around the nappy. It arched its back and dug its cold bare feet into Sprat's neck. "It isn't Russell at all...." He dropped the baby into Tanya's lap and fled.

Chapter Eleven

He tried to sneak upstairs without being heard. His dad followed him up and into his room.

"Where've you been?" he asked.

"I went to see a friend. She ... he ... she was out." He was conscious of the reek of sour milk on his shoulder.

"I want to talk to you, Sprat."

Sprat sat down at his desk and switched on his computer. "I've got this new game, Dad, with the money you left out. It's a flight simulation. Want to try it?"

"I said I want to talk."

"Actually I'm quite tired." Sprat switched off his computer and tried to yawn. "Really, really tired."

"I thought we'd been burgled at first."

"I'm sorry about the mess, Dad."

"I want to talk to you about Annie."

Sprat peeled his jumper off and tried to rub off the baby-sick smell with spit.

"Did you hear what I said?"

"You've never wanted to talk about her before," he mumbled between spits.

"What?"

"Why now? Honestly, I'm really tired, Dad."

His dad sat on the edge of his bed and watched him. "What're you doing, Sprat?"

"This baby puked up on me."

"What baby?"

"Caroline's. Not her's. Her mum's. I had to hold it while she rang up, I mean ... I was at her mum's when she rang up.... She wasn't there at the time...."

His dad smiled. "I'm sorry I haven't talked to you about Annie. I should have known you wanted to talk about it but it wasn't easy so I didn't."

"I don't want to. You're never here, anyway, if I did want to talk about it."

"I can't help that, Sprat. It's my job."

76

Sprat let his sweater drop to the floor. He really did feel tired now. He wanted to go to bed and not have to talk to his dad. He turned away from him and yawned loudly again, unbuttoning his shirt.

"So what do you want to say, Sprat?"

"Why didn't you tell her not to come?"

"She wants to see you."

"I don't want to see her."

He took his shirt off and put his pyjama jacket on. He would have to turn round to reach his pyjama trousers, still in their blue puddle on the floor where he'd dropped them that morning.

"I wish you'd look at me, Sprat."

"Why?"

"I find it quite hard to talk to someone's back."

"It's quite easy, really."

"Well, it's hard for me. I've been hurt, too."

Sprat stared at his bowl of goldfish. "She's gone now, and I've got used to it," he said at last. "She might as well stay away."

"It's not as simple as that, Sprat." His dad switched on his computer again. It bleeped into life. "I'd quite like her to come back, you see. Where's that game?"

Sprat's hands were shaking. He pulled open his desk drawer and flipped through his games cassettes.

"I'll get another chair, shall I? It's dead good, this."

His dad gave him a mock punch on his chin. "Bet I get the highest score. I was brought up on Biggles books, remember."

Tired though he was, Sprat lay awake for a long time that night. He was aware of things he'd never noticed before; his goldfish grovelling round the bottom of their bowl, displacing the stones noisily; the bright green glare of his digital radio alarm; the shuddering vibration of the fridge down in the kitchen.

He couldn't remember his mother's face.

Two mealtimes came floating into his thoughts; the first was during the Christmas holidays the year before last. His mother had said she had no time for Christmas that year, because she was studying for important exams. "Christmas will happen anyway," she'd said. "It always does, somehow." Christmas had happened, thanks, she'd said, to frozen turkey and Mrs Peake's Christmas pudding and television, but their real Christmas had come right at the end of the holiday, when her results had come through, and the promotion she'd wanted. He remembered the fizzy sensation of champagne coming down his nose, and his dad hugging his mother and swinging her round the front room so her skirt swirled out and she shouted at him to put her down.

"I can't lose my dignity now I've got my own ward to look after," she'd laughed. And she'd held her glass up to be filled again. "My career has begun!" she said. "And I'm thirty-six years old. It's been a long, long haul getting here."

Why couldn't he remember her face then, happy, laughing?

The other meal had been on the day of his parent's wedding anniversary, nearly a year ago now. He remembered the cooking smells and the crisp whiteness of the new table-cloth, the stain of red from spilled wine, the hurt silence while he and his mother waited for his dad to come home. He heard again the scrunch of tyres on the gravel that brought her into action; saw her sway slightly and hold her head as she bent down to open the oven, as if she was drunk, but her face was white and peaked. He remembered that. He remembered sitting alone in the dining-room, afraid suddenly, and not knowing why. He could hear the scraping of his knife and fork on the plate as he ate through his own meal alone; and voices upstairs, and a sudden burst of laughter that wasn't laughter at all from his mother. He remembered trying to drink from an empty glass when she opened the door and came in, ashen-faced, holding her bag, wearing her coat.

"I'm going to stay with Auntie Jean for a bit," she had said.

Sprat hadn't looked up then. He had smelt the pale flowery perfume of his mother's face-cream as she brushed her cheek against his.

He hadn't seen her since.

But why, even before his father had come home that night,

had Sprat heard her vomiting in the bathroom?

He had forgotten about that. It was important.

He sat up in bed, puzzled, about to put the light on, and then he sank back on to his pillow again.

"Because of the baby!"

At last Sprat fell asleep.

When Sprat got up the next morning his dad had already left for another business meeting in yet another town. Sprat remembered his mother crying about such meetings months ago – or was it years ago? He pushed the memory out of his mind. His mother was wrong.

Even so, he dressed in his newest clothes and washed his hair. He found a note by the kettle from his dad. "See you at five. Good luck, Sprat." He remembered the mess in the front room and went in to clear it, but the room was tidy again. The mantelpiece was bare, though. He picked some snowdrops from the back garden and put them in a wine glass. He realised that his hands were shaking. He paced round the house. He'd no idea what time she was coming. He had ridiculous ideas about tidying out the cupboard under the stairs, or cleaning the windows.

When the doorbell rang at last he was trying out suitable, interesting music on his cassette player. He turned it down at once, regretting his selection. The bell rang again as he went down the stairs. He saw a figure through the coloured glass of the front door.

"Hi Mum," he muttered. He had trouble opening the door. For some strange reason he couldn't control his hands.

"Come in," he said, pulling it open at last.

It was the milk woman.

"Has your dad left the money, love?" she asked. "It's a lot this month. You've had an awful lot of eggs."

"It was the pancakes," Sprat explained stupidly. "We forgot about Pancake Tuesday so we had a lot of pancakes that weekend. About ten, I should think."

"He hasn't left the money, then?"

"Not really. He's very busy."

"Tell him, love. He ought to know by now. Saturday's my day."

He shut the door and laughed to himself. Pancakes! They'd had to throw the frying pan away!

He ran upstairs lightly and didn't even hear the key turning in the lock. He came out of his room again when he heard a baby crying. His mum was standing in the hall.

"Hello, love," she said. "How are you?"

He stared at her. Her hair was different. She was wearing a coat he'd never seen her in before.

"I'm fine," he said. "Fine. I had a few cold sores, but they've gone now."

"Good."

She took her coat off and hung it over the newel post, just as she'd always done.

"I'm going to make myself a cup of coffee, love. Would you like some?"

"Yes, please. I don't take sugar these days."

"Good lad. Poison, that stuff. Should never have started you off on it."

She went into the kitchen and gradually Sprat came down the stairs. The bundle in the pram was something that had to be ignored. He dodged past it, daring it to start crying, and went into the kitchen. He was pleased that it looked so clean.

"What d'you think of your brother?"

"All right."

His mother laughed. "He's more than all right, you know. He's very like you."

"Is he my brother?"

"What do you mean?"

"I mean, really, is he, you know . . . is he really my brother?"

"Yes, love. Of course he is."

"I'll have my coffee black, please. The milk bill's rather high this month."

She handed him his cup.

"I didn't want another baby." She spoke as if she was just telling him about a day's shopping expedition. Her voice shook

80

slightly, he noticed. "For a time I didn't really think I wanted to be married. You have to stop and think about it, sometimes. You have to find out if it's still right for you."

"I suppose you do." He was too embarrassed to look at his mother. He sipped his coffee quickly and burnt his tongue because it was too hot. He breathed in sharply, folding his tongue to cool it.

The baby woke up and gurgled in the hall.

"D'you like him now?"

"Who?" She was miles away.

"Him. The baby."

"Of course I do. I love him."

Sprat felt a rush of jealousy. If it hadn't been for that baby, then, his mother would never have left home.

The baby gurgled again. The plastic mattress creaked as he pushed himself against the sides of the pram.

"I'm used to babies, you know," said Sprat. "They like me. My girlfriend's got one."

"That's useful," his mother smiled. "I didn't know you had a girlfriend."

"I'm just getting used to it myself. She doesn't know herself yet."

"Doesn't know what?"

"That she's my girlfriend."

"I see."

"It's not really her baby, of course. I only said that...." He was blabbering hopelessly. There was something he wanted to ask his mother but he couldn't find a way of saying it.

"Would you like to see him? His name's James. Jamie."

"In a bit."

"I nearly called him Adrian."

"Adrian! You wouldn't have!"

"I'm only joking. But it's such a lovely name, and it's wasted on you."

"No one calls me that, except Grandad."

"Well, perhaps you'll grow into it." She laughed. "I hope you haven't got much more growing to do. Taller than your dad now?"

81

"Jamie and Sprat. I like Sprat better than Adrian or Russell."

"Russell?"

"That's what her mother calls me."

The baby howled.

"I think I'd better feed him."

"I'll go upstairs, then."

"You don't have to, love." She said. She went out to the pram and lifted up the screaming bundle. "But you can if you want to. You'll have plenty of time to see him."

The bundle screamed again.

"I suppose that means you're staying," Sprat shouted, bewildered, half-way up the stairs.

His mother smiled up at him.

"If that's all right with you and your dad." She took the bundle into the kitchen.

Sprat ran into his room and did a handstand on his bed. He gazed round at the upside-down room till his eyes went funny. Then, feeling rather dizzy, he groped his way downstairs to have a look at his new brother.

Chapter Twelve

When the class came back after half-term, Nasim, always the first there, found herself alone in the classroom with Susan. Nasim had her books out ready and was working. She glanced up when Susan came in.

"Please can you help me? I don't understand."

Susan looked over her shoulder. "French!" she said. "I didn't think you were doing languages yet."

"Miss Quin said I must start now. It is very hard for me, though."

"I bet it is. What do you talk at home? English?"

Nasim laughed. "No, never! We usually talk Panjabi, but some people talk in Urdu with us. And I know some Arabic, too. My father want me to read Qur'an in its original language."

"Your English is fantastic, then."

"Thank you," said Nasim. "My teacher in Pakistan was an English lady. It helps me very much when an English person talks to me."

Susan looked away quickly, ashamed. It was the first time she had spoken to Nasim since the day in the changing-rooms, and she had never noticed any of the other girls talking to her. Mr Bead sat in the chair next to Nasim every morning after registration and talked quietly to her, and that had made some of the class feel jealous. She decided that she would make herself say something to Nasim every day.

It wasn't easy at first. She found it difficult to think of anything to say, and she felt self-conscious if she was found talking to Nasim when her friends came in. Sometimes she would just say, "Hiya, Nasim" and make that count. Nasim always gave her the same friendly smile, and began to look out for her.

One morning as Nasim was coming up the drive a couple of older lads shouted something out to her. She pretended not to notice and hurried on. "Oi, Pakki!" one of them shouted at her. "Look at me when I'm talking to you!"

Again she carried on. Her brother had told her that names

would never harm her, and she must learn to smile at them. She always did that, but it never eased the hurt she felt deep inside herself. She would never understand why people should want to hurt her. "Oi, I'm talking to you!" She looked up, startled, as one of the boys ran up the path to her and stood in front of her, barring her way. She stepped to one side, and so did he, and then again. She turned round and the other boy was standing right behind her. Some of their friends sauntered over, jeering, and within seconds she was trapped in the middle of a loud, taunting ring. She couldn't bring herself to speak or even to look at them, and the more she tried to break through the circle the more they laughed. They were shouting words at her that she only half-understood, but it wasn't the words that frightened her – it was their loud, jeering voices, and their laughing, hard faces. She put her hands over her ears and closed her eyes, and the only words that came to her were from the Qur'an, the holy book of Islam.

Susan and Donna walked past, ignoring the pushing ring, and then a sudden roar from the lads made them turn round.

"What are they up to?" asked Susan. "Can you see?"

Donna jumped up, using Susan's shoulders as a lever. "They've got someone in the middle. Hey, I think it's the new kid."

"Nasim?"

"Come on. They'll let her go when the bell goes," Donna said, uneasy. She'd been trapped by lads like this once; it was one of the most frightening things that had ever happened to her. "Leave her, Susan. They'll get you as well."

But Susan was running back to the group. She could just see Nasim's face as the lads danced round her.

"Leave her alone," she shouted. The lads didn't even turn round. "Leave her, leave her." She pummelled on someone's back. Nasim caught her eyes, lost, startled. In a wave of hatred Susan kicked out. "Let her go, will you! She's my friend."

Her shouts were drowned in jeers.

Donna saw Joe Bead's car edging slowly up through the gates and ran down to it. She banged on the window and he wound it down, smiling at her.

"They've got Nasim, Sir," she panted.

He saw the crowd at once, stopped the car and ran to them, shouting. As soon as the lads saw him they dispersed, like startled birds sent up from their prey, and Nasim stood with her schoolbag clasped in her arms, drooping slightly as though all the life had drained away from her.

Susan was shaking. She was surprised at the energy of her fury, and at the realisation that she had felt absolutely responsible for Nasim. There wasn't one other person in the school who would have done what she had done.

"Are you all right, Nasim?" she asked.

Nasim nodded, still too frightened and bewildered to speak.

"I'd better move my car," said Joe Bead. "I'm blocking the drive. Thank you, Donna. Thank you, Susan." He looked at Nasim but she couldn't bring herself to look at him. He wanted to apologise to her for the animal behaviour of those lads, but he didn't know how to do it.

"Look after her," he said.

When the lads ran off they were followed by Twagger. Although he hadn't seen anything of what had happened he'd seen the circle breaking up and Nasim, head bowed, in the middle of it. He dropped his satchel on the ground and hared after the lads, brought one of them down and pummelled him till he was hauled off him by Stan Murphy, the games teacher. The fifth year boy ran off and stood at a safe distance, laughing.

"I saw that! What's your name, lad?" Stan Murphy shook Twagger by the shoulders. "You're that Sanders kid, aren't you? Eh? You might be a skinny little rat but you're a real trouble maker. Aren't you? Now get lost before I teach you what real fighting's like."

Twagger backed away, wiping his nose on the back of his hand, gasping for breath, and then spat on the ground and ran off. Stan watched him, shaking his head, dimly remembering Joe Bead's strange question about bruises. "Any bruises that lad's got will be of his own making," he said to himself. "There are some people that no one will ever like, and he's one of them."

At break-time that day Susan came up to the front of the classroom and sat in the chair next to Nasim's.

"If you want to come outside, we'll walk round with you," she told her. "But if you want to stay in, I'll stay in too."

Donna nudged Caroline and Simone and they went shyly up to the front. "You all right, Nasim?" she asked. Nasim smiled at her. "Yes, thank you. It is very nice of you."

Sprat wanted to talk to Caroline. He hung about at the back of the group with Martin, then sat on one of the desks. There was a sense of occasion about everyone staying in at break, though he had no idea what had brought it about.

"Remember the igloo?" he said suddenly. The others laughed.

"It seems ages ago now," said Susan. "Doesn't it seem years ago, as if we were all little kids then?"

"Nasim wasn't even here then," said Caroline. "Go on, Sprat. Tell her about the igloo."

Joe Bead was on yard duty that day. He heard the roars of laughter coming from the mobile and, frowning, went across to see what was happening. He saw a group sitting on the desks, laughing, and in the middle of them Nasim, bright-eyed, turning her head from one to the other as they talked. Without anyone noticing him he closed the door to keep the cold out, and left them to it.

Susan and Nasim walked to school and back together every day after that. One wet and blustery day in March they stopped at the corner shop to buy some fruit gums. Nasim divided the tube up while Susan held her umbrella over them both.

"Don't you ever get sick of English weather?" Susan asked her. "I do. I'd move any day."

"I like sunshine very much," Nasim agreed. "But I like England too. We have a lot of rain in Pakistan anyway, at the end of the summer and in the winter."

"What will it be like there now?"

"It will be full of sunshine and sweet peas and marigolds," Nasim laughed. "Very lovely now."

"Have you been anywhere else round here, Naz? Up to

North Yorkshire or anywhere like that?"

"What is North Yorkshire?"

"The moors. It's really lovely. We go up most weekends, walking and that. You could come, if you like."

Nasim drew in a sharp breath.

"Your parents don't mind?"

"Of course they won't mind. Why should they?"

"I don't know why they should, but they might."

They finished the sweets off and stood at the side road where Susan lived.

"I'll ask Mum tonight, shall I? You'll have to wear boots, mind."

"I don't have."

"Doesn't matter. I've got some old ones you can borrow. They let in something rotten."

"What?"

"I mean they leak. Perhaps we won't go too far. Shall I ask?"

"Yes, please, Susan. And I ask my uncle. You are very nice," she said shyly. She watched Susan till she had turned the corner, then ran to her own house.

"Auntie! Auntie! I'm home," Nasim called, excited, as she pushed open the door.

"She's out," shouted Yasmine from the kitchen.

Nasim went in to her.

"Didn't she meet you from school, Yasmine?"

"Yes, but then she had to go somewhere."

"With my uncle?"

"Of course."

"She never out when I come home. Never."

Yasmine shrugged. "They go to make arrangements for you," she said.

"Arrangements? What arrangements?"

Yasmine turned away. "Can't say," she said.

Nasim took her wet coat off slowly. Her head buzzed with prickles of worry. What could be so important that her Auntie would leave Yasmine alone in the house and not be home for her when she came back from school?

"Tuhannon Bhok laggi hay?" She lapsed into her own language without realising it.

"Ji," nodded Yasmine.

Nasim put the grill on and started to make a quick toast snack for them both, their 'chaa' as they always called it. Spinach and potatoes were on the table, ready for the evening meal of saag, her favourite. Yasmine ate the toast before Nasim had a chance to get herself a piece. She would do without. She wasn't hungry now. She started to prepare the potatoes that her aunt had left out.

"Do you want me to tell you why they've gone?" Yasmine asked.

Nasim didn't answer. Her stomach was heavy with dread.

"Promise you won't say I told you."

Again Nasim was silent, her head bent over her work at the sink.

"Well, I won't tell you about the letter, then."

Nasim wiped her eyes with the back of her hand.

"You must tell me now," she said. "I am afraid they have had bad news about my Nanny-Ma Kauser."

"No," said Yasmine. "Not that."

She drank her tea noisily. Nasim flung down the potatoes that she was washing.

"*Yasmine!* Stop it. Tell me."

Yasmine slipped down from her stool and paraded round the kitchen chanting solemnly.

> "Your big brother
> has sent a letter
> to say you must
> go home and marry
> Zaffar Mohammad."

Nasim let the towel slip slowly from her hands. She went upstairs and washed herself and changed out of her uniform and dressed herself in the rose shalwar-kameeze that her Aunt Zarniga had just finished making for her. She was to wear it for Eid feast, in the summer. She searched out the gold-leaf earrings that her great-grandmother had given her, and carefully put them on. They dangled, gleaming against the black lustre of her hair as she brushed it out and replaited it. She had

88

all her silver and gold bangles on, and they jingled tinnily as she moved her arms. She looked at herself, at her smooth and perfect dusky skin and the deep chestnut warmth of her eyes, and knew she was a woman now. She draped her silk dupatta across her shoulders, and then wound it across her face so only her eyes could be seen.

Then she let it drop, gossamer-soft, into its glowing folds.

She went downstairs and Yasmine looked at her, surprised. These were not clothes to cook a meal in.

But Nasim wasn't going to cook a meal. She put her winter coat on again and went out into the swill of the rain. She was nervous. A muslim girl should not go out on her own in the evening, but it wasn't yet dark, she told herself.

If one of her sisters had done this when her father was alive she would have been beaten, and maybe even locked in her room. "But my father is not alive. My father has left me. I am not at home. I have been sent to England. And now I am not a child. I am a young woman, fit to be married."

In the rainy half-light of that evening Nasim felt as if she was floating between the secure world that was centuries old and that she knew so well as she knew herself, and a new one that she dared not imagine, one that shimmered as bright and fragile as ice-crystals. She was trapped in a dawn, or a twilight, like a photograph that just begins to take definition in its solution.

The rain increased in its intensity. She was too frightened to shelter in shop doorways, and she ran along the puddled pavements, ashamed now of the curious glances people cast at her as they hurried past. Almost without realising it she made for school, and turned with relief into the long quiet drive.

Water gushed from the roof of the mobile, swilling round the steps. She peered through the window, and could just make out the ordered lines of tables and chairs. How familiar her own table seemed now, pushed up against Mr Bead's desk. She could almost hear the scraping of chairs and the hum of voices, and Mr Bead's voice, intoning the register like a prayer.

"What d'you think you're doing here, this time of night? Eh?"

Mightymouth Mulloney's shout startled her. She didn't know

him. She pressed her back against the wall as he came across from the main building and scraped his feet on the step.

"Get yourself off home. I'm not interested in kids this time of night."

Without looking at her he unlocked the door of the mobile, thrust his head in, and locked the door again. He trudged back towards his bungalow. The lights were already on. It was nightime now.

As soon as he had gone Nasim ran back along the drive, splashing mud on her silk shalwar trousers. She was very frightened now that it was dark, but she wasn't ready yet to go home. She knew that her aunt would be looking for her, that it was time for prayer, that it was wrong for her to be out alone at this time of night. As she ran she could hear her feet slapping through puddles, and the rasping of her own breath, and from long ago the sound of her father's voice telling her the words from the Qur'an:

By the morning hours and by the night when it is stillest
The lord has not forsaken thee.

Chapter Thirteen

Nasim wasn't sure which house was Susan's. She hung outside till a woman came out to put some milk-bottles on her step.

"Please," said Nasim, "where is living Susan Derry?"

The woman stared at her, curious about her distressed and sodden state, and pointed to a house further up the street.

Susan's mother opened the door to her. "Yes?" She asked.

"Please, is Susan in?"

The woman could tell that the girl was upset. She asked her to come in and went up to Susan's room.

"There's a girl to see you," she said. "I think it must be the girl you were telling me about. The dark girl."

"Asian, Mum," Susan corrected her. "Nasim." She ran downstairs to her. "Hi, Naz!" she called. "Come on up."

Nasim was overwhelmed with shyness now she was actually in Susan's house. She had never been in an English family's house before. She stood in the hallway, confused, too embarrassed to look up at Susan. Nothing would motivate her to move forward and climb up the stairs.

Susan came down to her. "Naz? What's up?"

Nasim tried to speak but couldn't. Susan looked helplessly at her mother.

"Naz. Tell us. Has someone been getting at you again?"

"Surely not . . ." began her mother, but Susan interrupted her.

"You wouldn't believe it, Mum, some of those kids at school are pigs. Ignorant pigs."

Her mother came up to Nasim and put both her hands on the girl's shoulders. She could feel the child shrinking away from her.

"Do you drink tea, Naz?"

Nasim nodded.

"Well, I was just going to make myself a cup, so how about you and Susan going into the room there, where it's nice and warm, and I'll bring us all a cup of tea through in a minute." She steered Nasim through into the front room and gently closed the door on her and Susan. Her husband was washing the dishes in the kitchen.

"Who was that?" he asked.

"A little Asian girl, come to see Susan," she said. "She looks as if she's had a bit of a shock. Don't go in the front room for a bit, Tom."

"I wouldn't eat the kid," he grumbled.

"All the same. I don't think the girls are supposed to be in the same room as men, or something."

He stared at her. "Don't be daft. Anyway, what do you know about how they live?"

She sighed, deeply ashamed. "Nothing," she admitted. "Absolutely nothing. We've got Asian families living all over this town. And I don't know a thing about them."

When she took a tray of tea and biscuits through into the room a few minutes later Susan had draped Nasim's coat round a chair to drip. She was sitting by the settee next to Nasim, and both girls were staring into the mock dancing flames of the gas fire. She put the tray down and looked a question at Susan. She wasn't sure whether to stay. Susan shrugged at her.

"Are you a bit drier now, Naz?" she asked.

Nasim glanced up at Susan's mum and smiled. Since she came to England she had had to learn very quickly who to trust and who to fear.

"Is something the matter?"

Nasim smiled again. "Not really, Mrs Derry. I wanted to tell Susan that I have had some news from home, but it is very difficult for me to explain. But it is this. My family want me to go back home now." Home. Her throat filled with the word.

"Oh Naz! You've only just come," said Susan.

"Why do they want you to go home?" Mrs Derry asked. She poured out the drink, uncertain suddenly whether this was the way Nasim had her tea.

"They want me to meet the man they have chosen for my husband."

"Husband!" Susan laughed in her sudden embarrassment. "What for?"

Now it was Nasim's turn to smile. "For getting married."

"Married!" Susan's mother sat down. "How old are you, for goodness' sake?"

"Thirteen."

"Thirteen!"

Mrs Derry was as shocked as Susan was. The three drank their tea in silence.

"Are you sure there hasn't been some mistake?" She asked at last.

"It is the custom in our country," Nasim explained. "Many families like to marry their daughters at this age. We are women, you see. Women must be married. It is our custom. Our culture."

"But you're not in your country now, Nasim. You're in England. And it would be unthinkable for an English girl, a child of thirteen, to get married...."

"My family in Pakistan want it for me, and they arrange it."

"You mean you don't even know the man?"

"I know his name. Zaffar Mohammad. He will be very nice. My family will be certain to choose someone very nice."

"Did you know this might happen, Nasim, even though you'd come to England?"

"My father, before he die, he want it. He want me to be true Muslim girl and woman, like my mother. My uncle here, Uncle Assan, is wanting me to be girl of the west, he says. New girl, he is calling it. New woman. Like Susan."

"Naz. What do you want?"

The girl looked down quickly. "I must do as my family says. It is our custom. A daughter must obey her family."

"But what do you want?" Susan's mother persisted.

"I happy that I see my mother again, and my nanny-ma Kauser. I like to go home again."

"But what about getting married, Naz?"

"I must do as my family say."

Susan's mother sighed.

"I don't want you to go back," said Susan. "I've only just got to know you."

"You are very nice," Nasim said. "Two weeks ago, I wanted

to go home. I am hating England, I am frightened here. Now I am wanting to stay. I am wanting to see my mother, but I wanting to stay."

Susan shook her head. "I still can't believe it. Honestly. I can't take it in. It feels like you've just told me you're going to die."

Nasim laughed. "It's not so bad."

"Would you like more tea, Nasim?" Susan's mother asked, to cover up the girl's embarrassment.

"I must go home," said Nasim, worried suddenly. "My brother and my uncle will be very angry with me, to be out of the house at this time."

"Then we'll walk back with you," said Mrs Derry.

Nasim only lived in the next street. All the way there Susan was planning speeches. She would beg Nasim's uncle to let her stay in England. She'd tell him that she couldn't imagine anything worse than having to get married at her age. "It's cruel," she thought of saying. "Nasim's not a carpet or a piece of material to be taken to the market-place and sold. She has a right to choose for herself."

But when they came to the house Nasim's aunt was on the step looking for her. She called inside the house and she and her husband both came outside to meet them. Nasim ran into the house but her uncle and aunt shook Mrs Derry's hand warmly and thanked her for bringing Nasim home to them.

"You are very nice," the uncle kept saying, just as Nasim did, while his wife stood beside him and smiled at them. "We are so happy that Nasim has made an English friend."

"We should have said something," said Susan on the way back to their house. "They've no right to do this to her."

"They've every right," said her mother. "We've no right to interfere, Susan. I'm sorry for Nasim, but who's to say that the western way of life is right and the eastern way is wrong?"

"I don't understand why it has to be different, though."

"Customs are hard to break, and they're important. We have our Sunday dinner at six at night, and next door have theirs at

94

one. Who's right?"

"It's a bit more important than dinner times! And she's so clever, Mum. She told me once that she'd like to do Medicine. What chance has she got now?"

Her mother shook her head. She put her arm round Susan's shoulder and squeezed her. "Anyway, I'm not thinking of marrying you off just yet. We've still got a lot to do together."

"Mum," said Susan, suddenly remembering. "I told Nasim that I'd ask if she could come hiking with us on Sunday. Can she?"

"If she's allowed to," her mum reminded her. "Of course she can. She's a lovely child, Susan."

Child! she thought.

And she's off to be married.

Aunt Zarniga hugged Nasim that night. "I am very, very happy for you," she said. "If you like this man when you go to meet him, we can look forward to hearing of a wedding soon."

Nasim nodded and went upstairs. Her school books were still piled on her bed from when she'd come home. Slowly she put them together and packed them back into the school bag. In two weeks time she would be back in Pakistan. Dark inside her, velvet-dark, she held the mystery of her future.

Chapter Fourteen

It was March; blustery days of rain came to drive away the last of the snow from the streets, though it still clung to the edges of fields and the higher slopes of hills. People were beginning to think that spring would never come. Tuesday the tenth of March was Twagger's birthday. It began well. When he called in to school for registration Joe Bead had noticed the birth date on the register and wished him a happy birthday. Twagger scowled at him. "Fourteen bumps at break," Sprat said. "If you can catch him," said Martin. Twagger kept his fists clenched on the table and glared out of the window. "Don't bother," he muttered.

As soon as the register was finished and the class divided for their Latin and German he hurried off. He knew where he wanted to spend his birthday, and it certainly wasn't with M. Poirot. He sidled through the trees down the drive and was just in time to catch a bus down to the motorway sliproad. He had a couple of miles to run, and then he slipped over a stile that said "Access strictly by permit." He followed his familiar, muddy track back down towards the motorway. Two black and white horses trotted across the field to him. One of them had a black front that just looked like a bathing costume – it came down in two straps from the shoulders and narrowed in half way down and out again, and came to a neat curve at the top of its legs. He called her Bathing Belle. She lowered her head over the fence and nuzzled up to him. "Come on, me ould," he said to her. "What you been doing, eh? You don't half pong today." She swung her heavy head down and tugged at the grass between his feet. "See you." He called to her. He patted her veiny neck and carried on down the path. Sapling birches that had somehow survived the ice twisted in their protective cardboard gloves. A little throng of greenfinches hustled up and flung themselves away from him as though the wind had tossed them. He laughed and started running.

The path twisted back sharply before it reached the motorway and followed a fenced-off railway track, and then the trees became denser and higher. He slowed down and walked quietly, tuned in now to the many different birdsongs. He went as far as he dared. The field study centre was in sight. Any minute now one of the wardens would come out and send him off, though he never went far away if they did. He took his favourite path off to the left, leading over a little wooden footbridge where the papery white reeds whispered. He took a last look round, then climbed up the wooden steps of the hide, a hut on wooden stilts. He closed the door after himself, and breathed in the rich, sharp, familiar smell of creosote. The hide was in darkness except for narrow slats of daylight that just probed the line of shutters round the wooden walls. Twagger groped over to the high bench that ran down three sides of the hide. He carefully lifted up the long narrow shutter in front of him. It was a spy-hole on to the marshy pool. Grey March drizzle pitted the water, but here and there among the reeds he could make out the bobbing heads of wild-fowl. He undid the satchel that his mother had bought for him at a jumble sale last year, and lifted out his sketch pad and pencils, another present from his mother the day she left home. He opened it at the page which showed a dead elm on the right hand-side of the picture, and, very lightly, he began to sketch in the pair of pied wagtails that had just bobbed down to the edge of the pool.

Hours later, when school was over for the day, Sprat and Caroline sheltered under a tree near the school gates. It was raining again, and Sprat balanced his sports bag on his head to keep himself dry. Little rivers ran down the side of it and dripped on to Caroline's head, but she didn't say anything. She didn't really want him to move away.

"My mum's coming to pick me up today," she said. "Why they've gone and put cookery on the same day as orchestra I don't know. How am I supposed to carry a tin full of lemon meringue pie as well as my French horn and my games kit and my school bag?"

"We could always eat the lemon meringue pie," Sprat suggested.

"No way. It's our pudding tonight. It'll never go round six of us, though."

"Might as well eat it, then. Save arguments."

"Get lost."

Sprat turned his face up into the rain and whistled.

"D'you want me to ask her to give you a lift?"

"No, thanks," said Sprat. "I like getting wet."

Mr Bead beeped at them, smiling, as he nosed his car through the gates and round the puddles, avoiding splashing them.

"If we give you a lift we can pop into your house and see your baby," Caroline said.

"He's a pain," said Sprat. "All he can do is yell his head off and wet himself."

"I know. They're great, aren't they?"

"They're practically bed-ridden at that age, anyway. Dead boring."

Mrs Shepherd drew into the kerb and beeped gently. She wound down her window and waved at Sprat.

"Hello, Russell. D'you want a lift?"

"No, thanks," said Sprat. "I've got to pick up some stuff for our baby on the way home."

"I see. So you have got a baby. I'm glad you've made up your mind at last, Russell."

"It's not mine, it's my mum's," he tried to explain as she wound up the window again. "And I'm not Russell." But the car, with Caroline grinning inside it, had gone.

A woman who had been standing at the gates holding up a broken umbrella came over to him.

"Excuse me," she said. "You don't know a lad called Michael Sanders, do you?"

"He's in our form," said Sprat.

"I've been looking out for him for ages," the woman said. "You don't think he's gone already, do you?"

"He hasn't been to school today. He came first thing, but I haven't seen him since."

"Oh, dear." The woman frowned. "He must be ill."

"Probably." Sprat agreed. He turned to go, and then hesitated. "I could show you where he lives, if you like."

"No, thanks. I know where he lives all right."

Sprat wished Caroline was still there. He wanted to say "Are you Twagger's mother?" He knew she was. She had the same pale eyes. He felt a surge of anxiety and excitement for Twagger. Caroline was right, they had got something in common. He knew exactly how Twagger would feel if he saw his mother again.

By the time Twagger came home from the nature reserve he was soaked through. He'd walked back in the rain so he could spend the money he'd taken from his dad's pocket that morning. His trainers squelched with every step.

He started to run, worried in case the local sweet shop was already closed. He just missed his mother, who had been in to buy a card.

"I'll have a Mars bar," he told the assistant. "It's a birthday present."

Before he had left the shop he'd ripped open the wrapper and bitten into the chocolate.

Mrs Sanders hesitated outside Twagger's house. She shook her umbrella and let it fold up. She stood on the step and knocked softly. Water from the guttering dripped down onto her head. There was no answer. She tried again, and put her ear against the door. Nothing. She looked up and down the street to see if she could see anyone she recognised, then she quickly took her purse from her bag and found her key. She let herself in.

Old Mrs Heaton had had visitors that afternoon. It was her birthday too, and her son had come over during his lunch hour with one of her grand-daughters. They lived six miles away, yet she scarcely saw them from one month's end to the next. Her son was in a rush, as he always was when he came. He wouldn't settle down for a cup of tea. He paced round the room, making notes of things she needed doing.

"You could do with another plug point on that wall, Mum," he told her. "I'll fetch my drill and some cable next time. It'll only take me two minutes."

"You've not to go meddling with electrics, you know that," she said. But she knew he had no intention of putting in a plug point for her, and so did he. It was something to talk about, that was all. It made him feel better about not seeing her very often, and it made her think he cared.

She wasn't too keen on her grand-daughter. She was a giggly girl who wore too much make-up.

"Nan," the girl said, "I've got a present for you at home, only Dad said I couldn't bring it today."

"She doesn't want it, that's why," her father said. "What does an old lady want with one of them?"

"What is it?" asked Mrs Heaton. "A pair of ice skates?"

Sharon giggled. "Give over, Nan. You'd look daft. It's a puppy."

"A puppy?"

"Our dog's had its litter. Mam says we can't keep them and this one hasn't been taken yet. I don't think it will be, it's got a funny face. But she said it's got to be put down and I said that's cruel. I'd rather give it to me Nan, I said."

"Thanks very much."

"Will you have it?"

Mrs Heaton shook her head. "Your dad's right, Sharon. It'd be no good to me. I'd keep tripping over the thing."

"Please, Nan."

"Stop pestering her, Sharon, you heard her," her father said. "Come on, we'd better get back. Give your Nan that cake your mother sent and let's be going."

He gave his mother a hasty kiss and was off and out into the street before she had time to struggle off the settee. Sharon ran after him.

Mrs Heaton sat, quiet and pensive, after they'd gone. These rapid visits upset her. She'd rather they didn't come at all than this.

When home-time came she struggled over to the window, looking out in case Caroline happened to come, although there was no reason why she should on a weekday. She saw Mrs Sanders going past, and knew she recognised her from somewhere. A few minutes later she saw Twagger coming up the street, and she banged on the glass with her stick. He stopped and looked up, and she beckoned to him to come to the door. He waited in the rain while she fiddled with the bolt.

"What's up, Missus?" he asked.

"Nothing's up, love. I just wondered if you'd like to come in and have a piece of birthday cake with me."

He shoved his hands in his pockets. "How did you know?" he muttered, embarrassed.

"I had a good idea you liked cakes. All lads do."

"Who told you it was my birthday? Even my Dad's forgot."

"Your birthday?" Mrs Heaton looked at his thin, unhappy face. It's not right, she thought. Children shouldn't be unhappy. "Never mind who told me," she said, shuffling back to open the door wider for him. "Have I to put kettle on or not?"

Twagger made up his mind about her. "Yes, Missus," he grinned. "Yes, please."

Twagger's mother went straight upstairs to his bedroom. His bed was made, though his sheets were dirty. His room was as immaculately tidy as it had always been, and the walls were decorated with his drawings of birds. She stopped to look at one, thinking suddenly that she'd been there to admire it when it was first done. She doubted if he'd even shown it to his father. She sat down on his bed to write his card. 'Happy Birthday, love,' she put. 'All the best, Mum.' It wasn't enough, but she couldn't think of anything else. She slipped a ten pound note into the envelope and sealed it down. She had no idea what he'd spend it on. She didn't know what his interests were these days.

She went back downstairs and peeped into the mess of the kitchen. Her instincts were to tidy it up. She noted the pile of dented beer cans spilling out of the swing-bin. Maybe she would have a quick cup of tea before she went. She was soaked through, and had a long journey home to face. Besides, she might see the boy when he came home from school. There was a noise from the room as she went to fill the kettle, and she turned round to see the surprised and angry face of her husband

101

peering at her through the kitchen hatch.

"I thought you was out!" she said.

"What d'you think you're doing here, walking in as if you own the place!" he shouted.

"I told you. I thought you was out. If you don't answer the door how am I supposed to know you're in?"

"You wouldn't have come here at all if you thought I was in, more like. What you doing here, anyway?"

"Come to give the lad his birthday present, haven't I?"

"Come to make trouble."

"Don't talk daft. I'm his mother, aren't I? I got a right to see my son on his birthday."

"Well, he's out. So you can clear off." He settled himself back in his chair, angry and shocked at the distress he felt at the sight of his wife. "Why didn't you tell me you was coming?"

"It wasn't you I wanted to see," she muttered.

"What was that?"

"You heard. Look at the state of this place, Al. Honest, you ought to be ashamed of yourself, a grown man letting the place get like this."

"It's none of your business. You chose to move out. It's nowt to do with you now."

Twagger heard them shouting at each other as he was putting his key into the lock. The sounds were so familiar that it felt as if his mother had never been away. He ran upstairs and into his room, and his mother followed him up. He sat on his bed with his head bent down so she couldn't look at his face. He wouldn't open the card.

"Michael. You're all right, aren't you?" she asked him. Her voice was shaking. Her husband's rage, and her own, frightened her. She hadn't wanted it to be like this.

"I can't stop any longer, love. You can see that. I just wanted to have a look at you."

Still he couldn't look up at her.

"Are you going or do I have to chuck you out?" His dad's voice was thick with drink. He knew what would come next, and so did she.

"He doesn't hit you, your dad?" she whispered. Twagger shook his head. "Never let him hit you, Michael. But you stay with him, see? You're all he's got. It would break that man's heart if you walked out an' all. It would be the end of him, Michael."

Twagger flexed and unflexed his fist on his thigh. He watched the knuckle tighten and grow white. He counted in his head, very slowly, so the voice was louder than the sound of his dad shouting downstairs, louder than the quick rustle of his mother's bag as she bent towards him and touched his shoulder, louder than the sound of her steps running down the stairs, and the crash of the door that closed her out into the rain. Then he heard the voice screaming, "Thirty ... thirty one ... thirty two ... thirty three ..." as he ran down stairs and into the room where his Dad was bending down to switch on the television ... "thirty four ... thirty five ..." and the counting turned to sobs as he pummelled into his father's shoulder and into his surprised, swinging face and into the flat of the hands that rose up against him; and, as his father toppled down with his head hugged into his knees, his own sobs turned into the same loud, open, grieving moans that he could hear his father making.

Chapter Fifteen

The weekend was fine, for the first time for weeks. Soon after ten Joe Bead drew up outside Liz Peters's flat. She was looking out for him, and ran down as soon as she heard him.

"I've packed us some sandwiches," she said. "We should have a great day, if it stays like this. Have you brought a camera?"

He nodded. "And my binoculars. And my bird-book. I hope it's going to be worthwhile, Liz. There's a lot I could be doing today."

"Like what?" She teased. "Marking? Give up Joe, your brain will turn to jelly."

"I've got something to tell you," he said. "You know I told you I was thinking of applying for a new job?"

"I thought you'd forgotten about that."

"Oh no. I'm deadly serious. I've just been waiting for the right one to come along, and it has. I sent off an application before half-term, actually. I've been called up for interview on Monday."

She said nothing.

"It's in Snowdonia. I won't get it of course, and I don't suppose the boss would release me for next term even if they offer me the job. Anyway, I should have a nice day in Wales."

"Why didn't you tell me?"

"I didn't think I'd get this far."

"Snowdonia!"

"I won't get it, Liz." He drew up to red traffic lights and tapped his fingers impatiently on the steering wheel. "Would it bother you if I did?"

"What d'you think? How would you feel if I went and applied for a job in another school without even telling you?"

"I wouldn't like it," he admitted. "But I didn't know it would bother you that much."

The lights changed and he juddered forward in the wrong gear. The driver behind him beeped.

"You're a worse driver than me, Joe Bead," Liz said.

"Anyway, it's not a school," he said when he was in control of his car again. "It's a field centre. I've applied for assistant warden, arranging courses for hikers and climbers and . . . bird-watchers." He shrugged.

"You're leaving teaching!"

"I've had enough," said Joe. "Enough, enough, enough, Liz. I started off this term raring to go, full of ideas of things to do with the kids, things I knew they'd like, and gradually they've all worn down and all I can see is kids being nasty to each other and parents hurting their kids and teachers shouting at kids, and I've had enough."

"You're one of the best teachers in the school, Joe."

"And what does that mean? It doesn't mean I'm good at teaching my subject, does it? That's the last thing that matters. It means I'm good at keeping kids quiet and I'm good at talking to them and we all like each other and have a nice time in the classroom. Not any more, we don't. The classroom's the last place to get on well with kids, that's what I think. When they come to the field centre they'll be coming because they want to be there. We'll all enjoy it then."

"It's all to do with Twagger, isn't it?" Liz sighed.

"Yes, it is. And Nasim. And all the other little problems that have nothing to do with Geography or school or me. I've had enough, love."

"Calm down, Joe. We'll talk about it after. Let's promise each other we won't talk about school any more today. Don't let's spoil it."

They left their car in the car park of the nature reserve and walked slowly round to the willow pool. A couple of other people were already in the hide and training their binoculars on the water. For a time Liz was too upset about Joe's news to concentrate much, but gradually the peacefulness of the place worked through the turmoil that her mind was in.

Joe glanced at her as at last she brought her binoculars out. "O.K.?"

"Yes. I'm fine now," she said. He slid his hand across her shoulders. "Fancy thinking I wouldn't care," she whispered.

"Just fancy!" he said.

He scanned the pool and the banks with his binoculars, then stopped. He refocused them.

"What have you seen?" asked Liz. "Is the heron back?"

"Take a look at that, Liz," Joe whispered. "To the right of the clump of yellow reeds. What d'you think?" She focussed on the blur of a large shape, that became a bent figure crouching down by the side of the pool. The figure looked up, as if he could tell he was being watched. She lowered her glasses.

"I don't believe it, Joe," she said. "It's Twagger!"

Twagger had come into the reserve earlier that morning. He had sneaked in over the railway lines this time, and had spotted the lime-green armband of the warden too late to hide from him.

"Oi! You! It's you again. What d'you think you're doing! You'll get squashed by one of them 125's one of these days . . . ." He could hear the warden's voice as he ducked down into the bushes and ran doubled-up along the pathways that he knew by heart.

"I can still see you, you know!" the warden shouted. "I'll catch you one of these days. I hope I catch you before one of them trains does. . . ."

Twagger made straight for the willow pond on the opposite bank to the hide. He settled himself at last into the reeds and let his panting die down. The grey water rippled lightly as pochards dabbled near the reeds. A pair of shelduck ag-agged as they rose and dropped, chasing each other with their long slow wing-beats across the width of the pool. Twagger leaned back and grinned. This was the only place on earth he liked to be.

"Do we have to, Joe?" Liz grumbled. "Can't we just ignore him?"

"Of course we can't ignore him. If he's robbing nests he's got to be stopped."

"We promised we wouldn't talk about school today."

"I won't say a word about school."

Joe was striding in front in his eager, impatient way. She knew she'd either have to go with him, running to keep up with him, or sit in the hide and wait for him. Or else go off on her own.

She let him go and then, curious, followed him.

When he was within a few feet of where Twagger was crouching Joe started to creep. He could see that Twagger was hunched up over a clump of reeds, very near the water's edge. If he startled him the lad might even fall in. He paused very near to where the boy was sitting, and Twagger turned round, alarmed and ready to run. When he saw the teacher he raised his hand to silence him and then eased himself backwards till he was sitting at Joe's feet. Joe crouched down to him. Twagger was holding a sketch-pad. "Goldeneye, Sir," he whispered. As he spoke the bird skittered away from the reeds; raking the water surface with rapid whistling wingbeats. Joe tutted.

"Dun't matter, Sir. He always comes to this spot. I've done him now, I think."

"Let's have a look." Joe took the pad from the boy and looked at the sketch. "Marvellous," he said. "Didn't know you could draw, Michael."

"I can only do birds, sir. Get a lot of practice."

"Is this where you always come then, when you're twagging it?"

"Most days."

"Fancy that. Here's me thinking you're lounging round the Frenchgate Centre helping yourself to videos." It wasn't much of a joke, Joe thought to himself. Bit too near the truth.

"Like it better than school, do you?"

Twagger didn't bother to answer him. His head was turned up, eyes scanning the sky, as a couple of birds flapped across heavily. "Lapwings," he said, dismissing them. "Saw a hen harrier the other week. I heard it first, and I kept looking, and it never came, and I thought, this is it, I've had it now. It's never going to show. And then it just came up from those trees, and across the water, just like they did then. Long black fingers on its wings, like gloves. Never thought I'd see one of them here. Came right across, circling just over there . . . just coasting. . . ."

Neither of them heard Liz come. "What's he got, Joe?" she called.

Joe jumped up, and Twagger grinned up at her. "This is where you come to do your courting, is it, Miss?" he crooned.

"Don't be cheeky," she snapped.

"That's where they cuddle up, over in that hide. Lovey-dovey's in their nest ... know what it's called, that hide, don't you?"

"I did notice."

"Loversall Hide. I think it's rare good, that, because they all do! They all hide."

"Shut up, Michael. What are you up to anyway?"

"Bird-watching, Miss." His face was wide open with mock innocence.

"Raiding nests, more like."

"Too early for eggs, Miss. And they won't nest here, anyway. These are winter visitors. Should have gone, weeks ago. It's that long winter. Goldeneye shouldn't be here now. You're lucky to see it, Miss."

"Come on, Liz," said Joe, annoyed at her, and hating Twagger suddenly for his grinning impudence.

"That's right. You go and give her a cuddle, Mr Bead. Warm her up a bit."

Twagger laughed at them as they walked away from him. As soon as they'd gone he drew a line across his sketch of the goldeneye, and another, and then another.

Joe Bead and Liz went back into town soon after this. As far as Liz was concerned the day was ruined. Joe was tense and thoughtful as he drove back.

"Liz, I really think I've cracked it!" he said at last. "It's the first time ever I've talked to that lad and felt I've got through to him."

"Till I blundered up, you mean."

"Don't worry about that. He talked to me, that's the main thing. And I've found out enough about him to help him now."

"What with?"

"I've found out what he likes doing. Who'd have thought he comes down here when he twags off school? It never entered my head. He's not the lad I thought he was at all. He likes drawing, Liz, and he's pretty good at it. He's mad on wild-life. I know I can help the kid now."

"You mean you're going to follow him down here ever week like the good pally teacher and be his friend?" She was sarcastic, still sore because her morning out had been spoilt, and disliking Twagger for his insolent grins.

"It could come to that. I bet he could show me more about birdwatching than any of those books I've got on it. But I'm thinking past that, Liz. He's got a reason for coming to school now. Third-year options talks next week, and I know what I can talk to him about at last. He's got to take Art – I mean, perhaps no one's ever told him how good at it he is. You need to be told, don't you? And he can take Geography, and Biology. He's a natural for those subjects. He'll be all right. Once he finds out he can settle for the subjects that relate to the things he likes most, he'll like school."

"So it's all going to be cosy as a little nest in Mr Bead's class for nice little Twagger. And what happens when nice Mr Bead gets a new job in Wales? Who's going to bother about Twagger then? Not me, Joe. I'll do my job, and I'll teach the kid if he turns up, but I don't like him and I'm certainly not going to chase after him."

Soon after Twagger had set off that morning Mrs Heaton had ventured out of the house for the first time for weeks. There were days and weeks on end when she could scarcely move as far as her wheel-chair, and other days when she could get about quite steadily just with her sticks. On days like that she would exercise as much as she could, for the sheer pleasure of getting away from the prison of her house. Besides, today the sun was shining, or thinking about it, at least. The spikes of daffodil shoots were plumping out, yellow and promising, and birds were busy in gutters and hedgerows. Things were happening again. Mrs Heaton made her way steadily down the road, and when she reached Twagger's house she was struck with an idea that was so obvious and right that she felt a sudden rush of nervous excitement about it. She knocked on the door, and then on the window, with her walking-stick.

Mr Sanders was up early that morning. Since his wife's short visit he'd been edgy and bad-tempered. He found he could no longer spend his time just sleeping in front of the television set. He was aware of the dirtiness of the house. He went up to Twagger's room for the first time for months and was suddenly struck by its neatness. There, at least, nothing had changed since his wife had left. That made him angry and bewildered. He'd lost touch with his son. The bird pictures on the walls confused him. He had dim memories of taking the lad fishing, years ago, down by the canal, and watching a kingfisher teaching its young to swim. He remembered the child's absorption in it, and his own pleasure and puzzlement that such a tiny thing as a bird could seem so special.

When Mrs Heaton knocked he was trying to do something about the mess in the kitchen. The spill of empty beer-cans appalled him. He had no idea how to get rid of them all. He put as many as he could into carrier bags, thinking that he could maybe take them to the tip. He'd have to go on the bus. Everyone would know what was in the bags. Perhaps he'd send the lad with them instead. The knock at the door startled him, as if he'd been caught in an act of mischief. For a moment he thought it might be his wife again, and he pushed the bulging carrier bags under the kitchen table before going to answer it. He stared at Mrs Heaton, hardly knowing her.

"Is your lad in?" she asked.

He shook his head. "Has he done something?"

"No, love, course he hasn't. I just wanted to have a word with him, that's all. When will he be back?"

"How should I know? Never tells me anything."

"No. I don't suppose he does." She looked calmly at Mr Sanders. You're not going to bully me, her look said. You don't scare me with your bully voice.

"Was that Mrs Sanders I saw the other day?" she asked.

"Nosy old bag," he said. "What's it got to do with you if it was?"

"You're right," she agreed. "I am a nosy old bag. Can I come in for minute, Mr Sanders? I'm not used to walking about and my back's hurting. I could do with a sit-down and a cup of tea, if you don't mind. And I want to ask you to do me a favour."

Chapter Sixteen

"Michael. I'd like a quick word with you before you see Mr. Brown."

Twagger went up to Joe Bead's desk. He didn't say anything. It was the first time he'd seen him that week, even though it was now Wednesday.

"He's going to be talking to you about your options. You know that, don't you?"

Twagger shrugged.

"Well, he's going to be very angry when he sees your attendance record. He's going to expect an explanation for all these absences. What are you going to tell him, Michael?"

"I came on Monday. You were twagging it then."

"I was in Wales, Michael, and I had permission to be there. I don't just slip away from school when I feel like it."

"Bet you wish you could though, Sir," Twagger grinned at him knowingly. "With Miss Peters. I know where you get to, Sir."

"There's no need to talk to me like that, Michael."

"I know what you get up to, as well. Hiding in the hide. I saw you."

Joe Bead was tempted to snap at the boy and send him out.

"When Mr Brown asks you about your options, your choice of subjects –"

"I'll tell him I've chosen not to do any. He might have guessed that already, of course. . . ."

"Why don't you tell him that you're interested in wild-life, Michael? You could work at a place like the nature reserve one day."

"My dad's getting me a job at his firm, Sir."

"Michael. I know that's not true."

The interview was going nowhere. Joe Bead bent down to put his papers into his bag. "I think the subjects you might enjoy doing are Art, Biology and Geography," he said tightly, angry at the boy. He stood up again. "You'd like them, Michael," he said. "And I'd like you to do them."

But the boy had already turned away from him. Hands in pockets, he was slouching down to the door. "Can't stop here chatting all day," he said. "I've got a date with Mr Brown."

Nasim was just coming over from Main School when Twagger came out of the mobile. She smiled at him.

"Hello, Michael."

None of the kids called him by his proper name.

"What's your name again?" he asked her. "I've forgot."

"Nasim," she smiled. "It means Morning Breeze in my country."

"I've got something for you," he said. "I've had it a bit like, but I keep forgetting."

He pulled a screwed-up birthday card envelope out of his pocket and handed it to her. "There's a tenner in there. That's what I owe you for me jumper."

She unscrewed the envelope and took out the note. "I don't want."

"Me mother sent it to you," he said, scuffing up soil in the cracks of the path with the toe of his trainer.

Nasim nodded and put the note inside her bag. "I give it my uncle. He will be very happy now."

Twagger looked round him. It was too nice a day to stay indoors. He'd stay for dinner, he thought, and then he'd be off.

"Are you going for your interview?" she asked.

"Oh, aye. I'm going to do nuclear physics, me."

She took him seriously. "I was thinking I would like to be doctor."

"What did old Brownie say?"

"I did not tell him that. I am going home next week, you see. Perhaps I am going to be married."

He stared at her as if he'd never noticed her before, shook his head, whistling between his clenched teeth, and blew his cheeks out.

"Tough luck!" he said at last.

She smiled again. "Tuffluck? I do not know this. I think in Arabic they call it kismet. Destiny."

Joe had arranged to have a drink with Liz at lunchtime. She

112

left Caroline and Susan in charge of book club and hurried down the corridor after him. Just as they were going out of the building Mr Brown came in from the annexe. "Hang on, Liz," said Joe. "This is important. Sid, what options has Michael Sanders gone for?"

"Sanders?" Mr Brown shuffled through his papers. "Oh, him. Your little protegé. Have a guess, Mr Bead."

"Physics, Chemistry, Maths and Biology," suggested Liz. "He probably wants to be a brain surgeon."

"Wrong," said Mr Brown without a flicker of a smile. "I should have thought it was quite obvious to you, Mr Bead, as you know the boy so well...."

"Geography, maybe? Art?"

"Wrong, Mr Bead. He never even turned up. Twagged it, as they say."

"Come on," said Liz. "Let me buy you a drink, Joe, to cheer you up."

"I'm not surprised."

"Disappointed, though."

"Yes. Of course I am. I don't know where to go next. How can you help a boy like Twagger, Liz?"

"Nobody can."

They walked along in silence, threading their way through the traffic till they came to the pub.

"What happened about the job in Snowdonia, Joe? Have you heard yet?"

"I was going to tell you when I had a pint in my hand. I heard this morning. They've offered me the job."

"And – ?"

"An hour ago I couldn't make my mind up. But I know now, all right."

"You're going to accept it."

"Yes."

"I see."

"Don't say it like that."

"Well done," she said, flat. "A pint, to celebrate?"

He found two seats while she got the drinks. Her eyes were

bright. He tried to keep his voice steady.

"Liz, I want to ask you something."

"Have a crisp."

"Liz, I know you've got a lovely flat here. And a good job. You'll probably get a scale next year. You're a very good teacher. You like teaching here, don't you?"

"Have another crisp."

"I'm getting a house with my job. In Snowdonia."

"It would be," she said. "You could hardly commute from here."

"Listen, Liz. I wasn't going to say this yet. . . ."

"Mind if I join you?" A familiar whiff of stale tobacco floated over them as Mr Brown eased himself onto the stool between them.

"Wanted to have a word with you, Mr Bead, about the options your form have gone for. . . ."

Liz Peters moved away from him.

". . . now I've looked through them. Geography. They nearly all want to do Geography. It's not a competition, you know, to see who's the most popular teacher. You'll have to have a word with them to tell them . . . . Geography's all right of course . . . but it's not a serious subject, Mr Bead. Not a career subject. Wasting their time, unless they all want to be teachers, like us, eh?" He shouted with laughter, rocking the table and their drinks. He glanced from one to the other, waiting for their smiles. He pulled his cigarettes from his pocket. "Not interrupting something, am I?"

"No, no, it's all right," said Joe.

"Yes, you are, as a matter of fact," said Liz. "Joe was just about to ask me to go to Wales with him, I think."

The two men looked at her, drinks poised at their lips.

"And I was just about to say yes."

Twagger avoided Joe Bead and Mr Brown for the rest of that week, but he turned up to all his other lessons, a silent member, staring gloomily out of the window, lost in his own dark thoughts. When Friday came he arrived home in sunshine. Mrs

114

Heaton was making her way unsteadily down the street towards her house.

"Hello, love," she said.

"Hello."

"Been to see your dad."

"Have you?"

"Get on all right with your dad. Understand each other, we do. When my husband died I had a bad time getting over it. I know what it's like, losing someone."

"What d'you mean?"

"What I say, love. I took it bad over Fred, he's taken it bad over your mother."

"I don't know what you mean." Twagger tried to grasp the last sight of his mother, pale and quiet, dim as a ghost, slipping away. . . .

"You know what I mean. Your mum's left home for good. She's gone, duck. She won't come back. Face it. She had a hell of a time with him. There's no coming back for her. Face it." The old woman pushed forward with her sticks. "I've had a nice cup of tea with your dad," she said. "Don't like those teabags things, though. No flavour. "You can bring your own next time, Mrs Heaton,' he said. And I told him, 'Don't worry, Al,' I said. 'I will.'"

Twagger watched her hobble past him and up to her own house. He watched her lean her sticks on the wall and fumble for her key, and then heave herself up over her step and into her own dark, dusty house. Her door slammed to. He imagined he could hear her sitting down in her creaking armchair and sighing into the quiet of the room. He ran up the street and opened the front door of his house. His dad had the kitchen door open so sunlight was streaming through into the hall. He could hear him out in the back yard, talking to himself. He was about to sneak upstairs when his dad called through to him.

"Michael! Come out here a minute, will you? I've got something to show you."

The puppy stumbled on unsteady legs across the yard to Twagger. It was whimpering, a bit scared, a bit friendly. It had two black eye-patches that made it look as if it was wearing sunglasses. Twagger's dad was sitting on his haunches coaxing it, laughing at it.

"Eh?" said Twagger. "Where'd this come from?"

"Belongs to old bag up road."

"Her with sticks?"

"Aye."

"What's it doing here then? Dad, what you doing with her dog?"

The puppy stumbled up against Twagger's trainer and tugged at the laces. He knelt down to it, touched its throbbing side. He looked up, laughing. "Eh! Look at this!"

"Old girl wants you to look after it for her, for a favour, like."

"Look after it? Like what? What's she mean, Dad?" Twagger could hardly keep himself from grinning at the tininess of the thing as it stumbled past him and over to his dad.

"Wants to take his specs off, then he'd see better," his dad chuckled.

"What's she want me to do with it?"

"Told you. Her grand-daughter give it her for a present. Well, she can't see to it, can she? Can't get about too well. She asked me if you'd look after it for her, feed it like, take it for walks, you know. She's paying for its Doggo, like, all fair."

"So it's sort of mine?"

"Sort of yours and sort of hers. Taken a fancy to you, that old biddy has."

"She's taken a fancy to you an' all. She tells me she comes and has cups of tea with you."

"She's a nosy old kipper but she means well. Aye, she's all right. Lonely, stuck in there all day."

Mr Sanders stood up suddenly and wandered back into the kitchen. He got himself a can and sat down in front of the television. Outside he could hear Twagger larking about, larking about like a little lad with the patchy dog. Larking like a real kid.

Chapter Seventeen

"Before you all go dashing out I've got something to tell you," Joe Bead said. He'd been looking at his watch while the class had been clearing out their desks. Five minutes to go before the last bell on his last day of term. He wasn't looking forward to this bit. The class looked up at him. "I'm leaving," he said bluntly. "When you come back, you'll have a new form teacher and a new geography teacher."

"Oh, Sir, all the best teachers go," wailed Caroline.

"That's not quite true," Joe Bead said. "You'll still have Mr Brown, and Miss Grace...." The class groaned again.

"What about Miss Peters, Sir?" asked Martin.

"What about her, Martin?"

"Is she leaving too?"

"Well. I'm hoping so. But not yet."

"Are you getting married, Sir?"

"We might."

Some of the girls giggled.

"Flippin' heck," grumbled Martin.

"Mart's been running a book on it, Sir," said Sprat. "Think you'd better run for it, Mart."

"Anyway, I just wanted to say it's been nice teaching you, and I know you won't believe it, but I'll miss you lot...." His eyes moved round the class. Sprat, Martin, Matt, Stuart. Nasim's chair empty. Caroline, Susan, Donna, Simone ... He risked a glance at Twagger, and the boy caught his eye and looked down again quickly.

"Why didn't you tell us before, Sir? We could have bought you a pen or something."

He laughed. "I didn't really know for sure myself till now. You can't usually be released from school so soon, but technically we're overstaffed here. Perhaps the head was glad to get rid of me. Anyway, you gave me a pen for Christmas."

The bell went and the chairs were scraped back. "Bye, Sir," some of the voices chorused, awkward. "Thanks."

"Bye." He smiled.

"Won't we ever see you again, Sir?" said Donna.

"Oh, I wouldn't bank on that," he told her. "Off you go. Have a nice Easter."

Within seconds the classroom was empty. He wandered round, uselessly and unnecessarily straightening chairs. When Liz came in he was standing, hands in pockets, looking out of the window at the thin boy making his solitary way across the field to his house.

"Twagger?" she asked. Joe put his arm round her and drew her to him. They stood together, watching the lad's slow progress.

"He's got to make his own way," Joe said. "Nothing much is going to change for him, Liz."

"Did you tell them?"

"I did. They didn't exactly burst into tears."

"What did you expect? They've got far more important things happening in their lives."

"Funny thing," said Joe. "I nearly did."

"Sprat," said Caroline, "Come to Thornton's with me."

"What for?" said Sprat. "I'm supposed to be looking after our Jamie after school, so my mum can get out."

"Please. It'll only take five minutes."

He waited outside the shop for her, impatient and embarrassed.

"By the way," she said when she came out. "You owe me a pound. You don't mind, do you?" She opened the box she was carrying. "Look!"

" 'To Mrs Heaton,' " Sprat read. " 'From Sprat and Caroline.' Hell, Caz!"

"You don't mind, do you? If you don't want to, I'll pay it all, but you'll have to lend me . . . ."

"It's not that," he said. "What's an old lady want an Easter egg for?"

"Don't be soft," she said. "Why shouldn't she have an Easter egg, just because she's old?" They walked along in silence. "Maybe I should have asked," said Caroline. "I ordered it last week. It seemed like a good idea at the time."

118

A sudden gust of warm wind sent papers scuttling along the gutters. Sprat pushed his hair back away from his eyes. "Look. at you," he said. "You look like a horse with that hair."

"Thanks, Sprat." He smoothed her hair down behind her ears. It was the first time he had ever touched her, and his hands felt heavy and clumsy. His throat ached.

"Thanks," she said again.

"It's the words," he tried to explain, and his traitor voice cracked to falsetto. "Did you have to put those words?"

"What words?" She looked into the egg-box. "I could have put 'From Russell and Caroline,' I suppose."

"Great," he said. "You're as bad as your mother."

"I suppose you just didn't want to be seen on the same egg as me."

"Something like that."

"Your mum'll be waiting."

"Well, it looks ... you know."

"You'd better go."

"Don't be like that. You know what I mean."

"No."

"Hell."

"You're my best friend. That's all it means."

"Good."

"See you, Sprat."

"Righto."

"Next term."

"Right." She turned and walked away quickly. Suddenly his throat was tight again.

"Caroline – "

She turned round. Her thick hair splayed up round her eyes.

"When are you taking it to Mrs Heaton?"

"Sunday morning."

"Meet you there, then."

"Right." She grinned. "Thanks, Sprat."

He raced home with the mad March wind pounding his chest like tiny happy fists.

Nasim's plane took off into racing clouds, then soared through them into blue. She saw green fields and pink houses far below her, sliding out until they became the sea. She closed her eyes. Maybe she would never come to England again. It would depend on her husband now. She would like to show him the green moors of North Yorkshire. She would like him to come to school with her, and sit in the desk next to her maybe. . . .

She would write to Susan as soon as she got home, she thought, and tell her what she had found out about the man she was to marry. "I hope he is kind," she thought. "That is the only thing that matters."

Twagger made straight for the back yard when he got home. His father was out, but he'd made an effort to clean up the kitchen before he went. The puppy was whining outside, shoving the tip of its nose through the crack in the door. Twagger picked it up carefully and carried it into the room.

"Time for you to see the world," he told it. "It's bigger than our back yard out there. Look, I've got a pressie for you." He fished a collar and lead out of his pocket and slipped it round the dog's neck. The puppy squirmed, hating it.

"Come on, Scragg, let's get you out before me dad gets home and shouts at us."

Twagger picked up the dog and went out with him, back towards the empty fields by the school. A cluster of dusty sparrows sprayed up as he ran at them. He set the dog down and held tightly to the end of the lead. "Come on," he coaxed it. "Don't be scared. Trot about."

As the dog picked up courage Twagger walked along with it, and then ran. Soon the two of them were racing round the field, with Twagger leaping over the lead as the puppy scampered in circles round his feet.

Joe Bead saw them as he was walking to his car. He put his bag down and ran across to them.

"Twagger!" he shouted.

Twagger waved to him.

"Is it yours?" Joe Bead bent down to stroke the puppy, then jerked back as the dog leapt for his tie and swung on it.

"Sort of," said Twagger. "I'm looking after it. For a friend."

"Is that right?" Joe stood up, and the dog tumbled back away from him. "Clumsy little chap, isn't he?"

"He means well, Sir. He's being friendly."

"Has he got a name?"

"I don't know what the old lady calls him. I call him Scragg sometimes. He's a right mess, isn't he, Sir?"

Twagger twisted the lead round his wrist. He would have liked to tell Joe how sorry he was that he was leaving. He could see Liz Peters waiting by the car. He looked away, narrowing his eyes.

"Tell you what I'd like to call him, Sir. I fancy calling him Mr Joe, really."

Joe laughed, pleased. "Mr Joe, eh? I like that!"

Twagger knelt down and rubbed the puppy's back. "Come on then. Let's go and tell your old lady." He ran a few yards with the puppy tumbling behind him, then he bent down and picked it up. He danced round to face Joe.

"See you then, Sir!"

"Off you go. Leave me to my peace and quiet." Mightymouth Mulloney swings the school gate shut behind Joe Bead's car and bolts it down. "Can't say I'll miss you all," he says, making his way back to his bungalow. "Much."